DOWN, BUT NOT OUT IN HIGH SCHOOL

Written by Amy Berkowitz

A SISU BOOKS PUBLICATION

Down, But Not Out In High School
Copyright © 2010 by Amy Berkowitz

Published by Sisu Books Publishing
Sparrowbush, New York

Attention schools, educators and other organizations: Sisu Books makes titles available at a discount for educational, promotional and other events. For information please contact mworden@sisubooks.com or write to:

Sisu Books
PO Box 421
Sparrowbush, New York 12780

Visit www.sisubooks.com for information on other titles available from Sisu Books.

To contact the author:
amywriter@hotmail.com

Cover design by Gordon Bond
www.gordonbonddesigns.com

ISBN 978-0-9842283-2-4
Sisu Books Publishing

DEDICATION

This book wouldn't be possible without support from my family. My parents Harold and Shirley Berkowitz are my best editors and mentors.

My sister, Ellen and her husband, Steve, always wanted me to write for kids and their encouragement proved to be the most valuable tool I needed to accomplish my goal.

My niece and nephew, Rianna and Carson are my little test audience. I hope to make you both proud.

My friends: Eileen Foley, Susan Fydrych, Maggie Walsh and Tara Thomas, who allowed me to extract pieces of their personalities for these characters and also served as gentle readers.

Thanks to several teachers: Tony Battista and Jean Bolton, who encouraged me to choose writing as a career instead of science. They found opportunities to allow me to recognize my true calling and scientists everywhere can breathe a sigh of relief. My colleague and friend, Chris Farlekas, whose writing I always admired.

Thanks to the late Janis Osborne, former editor of The Gazette for giving me my first full-time reporter's job and introducing me to the charming little city of Port Jervis, New York. It made Kellie's world a lot easier to recreate.

Thank you to Sisu Books and Michael J. Worden for giving me the chance. To Walt Papalo and Erwin Benz of Into The Weekend with Walt And Benzee radio show on WTBQ and Lisa Ann Riccardelli for leading me to Mike Worden. To Gordon Bond for his beautiful cover design.

Special thanks to Kimberley Thompson from Stafford Labs Orthotics and Prosthetics in Goshen, N.Y., for explaining how they fit and care for prosthetics.

Finally, through my newspaper stories at the Times Herald-Record, I have had the pleasure of meeting many disabled children. They have showed me what the words "courage" and "perseverance" truly mean. Kellie could have never have come to life on these pages without you.

CHAPTER ONE

SCHOOL IS HELL ON WHEELS

Math is the last final to conquer before freshman year is over and the toughest one for Kellie Jones.

"Damn, not listed. I hate multiple choice tests."
Her hand cramps up as she flips her pencil to erase the answer to the last question on her scrap paper.

"Five more minutes." said Mr. Battista, her math teacher, who could do The Trachtenberg System with his eyes closed, but had difficulty walking across the room without tripping.

"This better work." she said to herself as she scribbled the problem down praying to become a math genius in the next few minutes.

"Yes!" Kellie put her hands up in a victory sign then quickly lowered them when she saw 23 pairs of eyes on her.

"Miss Jones," said Mr. Battista in a deadpan voice. "I'm so glad my Math class has finally made you happy even if it took the entire school year."
Giggles from the center of the room made Kellie blush.

"Now please put your pencils down and close your test booklets." Mr. Battista straightened his glasses. "After you pass them from the back to the front of the room you may leave and enjoy your summer."

The spine chilling screech of metal desk chairs against the floor sounded like a symphony to Kellie as she rolled out the classroom door into the crowded hallway.

"Kellie, wait for me!" Mrs. Connolly, her aide got up from her chair outside and waddled down the hall waving a newspaper in her hand.

Kellie's parents hired Mrs. Connolly to escort Kellie from class to class and Kellie made it her mission to ditch Mrs. Connolly as much as possible. She became really good at it too all those swimming lessons before her accident gave her powerful arms. Kellie cut through the crowd like she was driving Danica Patrick's race car.

"Hey, watch where you're going!" said a girl with a squeaky voice.

"This isn't the Indy 500, "Wheelchair Girl,'" said a deep male voice.

"Wheelchair Girl" – was her name at Port Jervis High School not Kellie Jones. To the other students she was just an obstacle in their way.

"Just roll the wheels a few more times and it's onto the elevator to freedom." Kellie thought as Mrs. Connolly's voice disappeared in the noise of the crowd.
The elevator door opened and no one was inside.

"Yes! Two more floors and I don't have to look at these people for two whole months."

Maggie and Kellie are fraternal twins that came to Port Jervis High School this past February. They lived their whole lives in Oneida, N.Y., where they were known as the "Twincesses".

After Kellie lost the lower part of her leg in a car accident, the twins' parents decided to start a new life where no one would know them so that Kellie could get a fresh start.

As for Maggie, she really didn't want to spend her freshman year in a new place. It was hard enough to start high school now she had to make all new friends too. She and Kellie shared everything, but Maggie kept this secret to herself.

Kellie rolled into the open elevator and pressed the button to close the door before her aide; Mrs. Connolly could make it through the crowd and get into the elevator with her. The lady was nice but she was constantly on her ass.

"Sigh! I just want her to leave me alone at least for two floors." Kellie whispered to herself. Anyway, the exercise would be good for Mrs. Canoli. Kellie smiled as she thought of the name Maggie gave rolly poly Mrs. Connolly, a large woman with blond curly hair and chubby cheeks. To Maggz (that's what Kellie called Maggie) she looked like she ate too many canolis. Mrs. Connolly meant well, but Maggie and Kellie couldn't stand the way she started every sentence with a patronizing "Now, Kellie."

Kellie rolled out of the elevator happy to see the area around her locker was clear. A few blond layers of hair fell from her pink pony tail holder as she opened her locker door and grabbed a mirror she kept inside.
Kellie rolled her eyes and said under her breath, "Great, girl you look like a total freak."

Wham! The force of a ball knocked her forehead against the metal door.

"Hey look where you're..." Kellie was interrupted.

"Aw, man I'm so sorry. Are you okay?"

Kellie's face twisted into a scowl as she turned to the right and saw a tall, lanky guy holding a soccer ball. Her face softened starring at his strawberry blond short spiky hair and flashing blue eyes. It was Eric Green, the soccer star, "King of P.J. High". Even Kellie, who didn't get involved in the social aspects of school, knew she was in the presence of royalty. She didn't know whether to yell at him or spit polish his cleats.

Here was her chance. Should she chew him out? He deserved it. Should she burst into tears and hope for sympathy? Lecture him on hall safety? Nah, she would sound too much like a mom. Kellie opened her mouth hoping something magical would come out.

"Yeah," was all she could say.

"Yeah what?" said Eric with one eyebrow up.

"Yeah, I'm okay." She said a little cranky, but the words seem to roll out without her brain giving a signal.

"Good. See ya 'round." Eric grabbed the ball and kicked it down the hall, picking it up just before a cranky hall monitor rounded the corner.

Kellie looked in the mirror again and rubbed her forehead.

"YEAH, I'M OKAY? That's all I could say? Stupid, stupid, stupid."

"Kellie, are you all right?" Mrs. Connolly put her arm on Kellie's shoulder.

"I'm just terrific! Great, brilliant, couldn't be better," she sighed.

Mrs. Connolly handed her a second box to put her books in.

"How was the test?"

"I bombed it."

"Oh come on, I'm sure you did fine. You studied for three weeks what makes you think you failed?"

"My new pencil has no eraser on it now."

"Well, maybe you did better than you think. Listen, you don't have to worry about it until the report card comes. Now, put all your school stuff in here and I'll take the box out to the mini van for you."

"I can do it myself." Kellie let out a puff of air trying to get her bangs out of eyes. Put it on my lap and let's roll."

4

"Now Kellie, let's not fight. It's my job to help you."

Too tired to argue she gave Mrs. Connolly the box.

CHAPTER TWO
JADED

"I'm going to run out the side door and put this box in the van. So wait by the front entrance and I'll come and get you."

Kellie sighed, "Ok", inside she wished she could "run" out the door herself.

Mrs. Connolly lumbered out the door and Kellie began rolling down the long hallway.

"Hey Tripod! Can't you roll any faster? Keep this up and summer will be over," A chorus of laughter erupted behind her. Kellie didn't even have to turn around to know that Jade Santiago, the head cheerleader and her "Jaded" girls were laughing at her.

Jade was "the perfect girl" with dyed blond streaks in her long curly hair. Her nails were painted in the school's colors of purple and silver. Kellie thought she was perfect all right, perfectly pathetic picking on kids that couldn't defend themselves. Jade was only kind to teachers and the Jaded girls, who dressed like her and worshipped her every move especially, Sora Hayashi, who came here from China. She was quickly added to the Jaded crew probably because she was smart. Jade would rather spend her studying time thinking about how to cheat on tests rather than learn the material.

"Just a few more yards and I'm golden." Kellie said to herself.

Maggz and their friend, Susan, waved at Kellie from the end of the hallway. Eric is Jade's boyfriend and Kellie experienced Jade's mean streak first hand when Eric showed her how to spin a basketball on one finger during a game. They were having fun until Jade saw them.

"I said move it." Jade took the handles of Kellie's wheelchair and pushed her into the wall.

"Hey!" said Maggie as she and Susan ran up the hallway towards Kellie.

Kellie's surprised look changed to relief after hitting the wall. She fully expected something to happen. Once, Jade put gum on Kellie's wheels at least Kellie thinks it was her. She has no proof, but she was pretty sure. A few students were called down to the nurse's office for an eye test. While Kellie and Jade were waiting on the long line for their test, Mrs. Connolly went to the restroom. Kellie was in front of Jade. She could hear her smacking her chocolate mint flavored gum.

Later that day, Kellie wheeled herself out the door. That's when she got chocolate mint gum all over her hands. Now, you can run over one wad of gum, but two wet pieces carefully placed on the back of each wheel? That's pretty doubtful.

"Are you OK?" said Susan, whose big blue eyes were open wider than Kellie had ever seen them. Susan moved to P.J. two years ago from Brooklyn. Susan is tiny, however as small as she is, no one messes with her friends.

"Hey Jade, What's your problem? In a rush to spray the fungus on your big, smelly feet?" said Susan with one hand waving in Jade's face while the other was stuck on Susan's hip. A head taller than Susan, Jade looked down to shout back.

"Listen Brooklyn, go back to the sewer you crawled out of."

"I'll give you a piece of Brooklyn," raising her left fist to Jade's face and tugging her hair with her right hand.

7

"Ow, stop it sewer sludge." said Jade trying to grab Susan's fist.

Mrs. McCoy, a popular teacher, ran down the hallway. "Hey, hey, girls it's the last day of classes. No need to start September off with a suspension. Move along now."

"Mrs. McCoy she started it." Jade faked some tears.

"I don't care, who started it. You're finishing it now."

Jade recovered from her tears quickly. "Come on girls we have more important people to talk to."

Kellie hugged Susan around her waist. "Thanks Suz, I'm glad you've got my back, but you better watch it. I don't want you to start off next year with detention."

"No biggie, when it's for a good cause. You know, they're some really cool people in detention, but you two wouldn't know that since you are rule abiding good girls." Susan rolled her eyes. "It's all so disappointing."

They laughed as they approached the front door. Maggie was first to hold the heavy glass door for Susan and Kellie.

"Hey Kell, we're gonna hang out at Riverside Creamery. Wanna come?" said Maggie. "I called mom and she said it was OK. We can stop home first and unload the locker stuff from Mrs. Connolly's car."

"I don't know Maggz. I'm trying to get away from the kids here, not hang out with them." The real reason Kellie didn't want to go to the creamery is everybody liked to sit on the tall stools at the lunch counter. Sitting in her wheelchair at the counter forced her to view everything like a two-year-old. She was so low to the ground she could only see the metal bases of the stools while everyone else could see above the counter.

Maggz knew what was on Kellie's mind. "We'll sit at a table."

"Yeah, Kell, I'll sit which ya when I get a break. I can't sit at the counter in my 50s poodle skirt get up anyway. It will give me a muffin top," laughed Susan pulling on the nonexistent lump of skin around her waist.

Then Susan added the clincher, "I heard Eric is going to be there."

Kellie began to blush.

CHAPTER THREE

SUSAN'S SADNESS

"Come on girls, hop in," said Mrs. Connolly as she drove up to the curb in her dark blue mini van. "You too Susan, it's too hot to walk to Lyman Street."

"Thanks Mrs. C., but I have to go right to work at Riverside Creamery."
Fine, I'll drop you off there."

Kellie knew Susan was relieved otherwise she would have to walk home, get her bike, and pedal three miles to Water Street. It must be hard working after school, but her mom needed her to help out with the bills. Susan would be working a lot now that school was out.

"This air conditioning feels so good," said Susan as she absorbed it like a sponge. "All mom and I have are two fans in the apartment and since we rent the top floor of a two-family house we get roasted like chickens each summer. Our old house in Brooklyn had central air and you could always go to Prospect Park at night for a concert. I really miss Brooklyn."

The twins knew her dad died two years ago. Susan and her mother left Park Slope, Brooklyn for Port Jervis and they were still adjusting. The wood-framed two story homes with wrap-around front porches on large lawns in Port Jervis looked nothing like the three story, Sesame Street- style Brownstone homes with wrought iron fences crammed side by side in her Brooklyn neighborhood. After her father died it became too expensive for them to live there. Her mother, a cute little Polish lady in her forties, spoke broken English cleaning hotels for a living. Her father spoke English a little better than her mom.

Maggie took a sip from her water bottle and saw a tear roll down Susan's cheek. "Hey, what are you cryin' about? It's the last day of school you should be ecstatic!"

Susan roughly wiped a tear that fell on her cheek, "Nothin', just thinkin' about my dad. You know it's strange, I always worried that he would fall on the job washing windows on those big skyscraper buildings. Instead, he is hit by a drunk driver while walking home from the Subway. It just never made any sense. He was such a good dad."

Susan's father was a short and stocky man. She remembers him as a hard worker washing the windows of the most famous sky scrapers in the city. He also had a soft side, an easy smile and he was always ready to give a hug. They had the prettiest Brownstone on the street because he loved to plant flowers in their little yard. Flowers were everywhere in the spring and summer red, yellow and magenta all popping up around the front stoop and behind the iron fence. But the flowers Susan remembers most were the ones she put on his casket.

Mrs. Connolly broke the silence.

"So what's the latest flavor over at Riverside Creamery? Mr. Reynolds is always coming up with the craziest concoctions."

"I think the latest is called piñata," said Susan. "He takes vanilla ice cream and chops a small jalapeño in it and stirs in rainbow sprinkles then he serves it in a dish that's shaped like a Mexican hat."

Kellie scrunched up her face. "Yuck, that's gross."

"It's not bad, the ice cream is like sour cream it calms down the spicy taste of the jalapeno. You should try it."

"No thanks," said Mrs. Connolly. "I think I'll stick to my usual favorite."

"What's that?" asked Maggie then she took a big gulp from her water bottle.

"Holy Canoli."

Maggie choked on the water. Kellie turned around in the front seat and gave Maggie a stunned look while Susan smacked her on the back.

"Maggie dear, are you okay? Do you want me to pull over?"

"She'll survive, Mrs. C., she'll survive," said Susan.

CHAPTER FOUR

GOOD NEWS DOESN'T TRAVEL FAST

Mrs. Connolly dropped Susan off at the creamery and drove two blocks over to the twin's home on Thompson Street so that they could drop their back packs off.

The girls thanked Mrs. Connolly and went into their house, a white two story Victorian. The house had eight steps leading up to the front wrap-around porch so their dad hired someone to build a ramp for Kellie on the side of the house.

Maggie ran to the mailbox and put the mail on Kellie's lap then she pushed Kellie inside the doorway.
When they got inside, they quickly said goodbye to Mrs. Connolly and greeted their mom. They put down their backpacks in the dining room and started to go upstairs.

"Wait just a minute my twincesses," said their mother, Shirley. "How did you do on your tests?"

"Great. English was a breeze," said Maggie grabbing a cookie from the plate on the dining room table. "The essay question wasn't as bad as I thought it would be. They asked us what modern changes in Romeo and Juliet would help stop the feuding between the Capulets and the Montagues.

"So what did you write?" said Shirley as she grabbed the stack of mail from Kellie's lap.

"I wrote that if their clothing wasn't as stiff and made out of comfortable material; they would be able to sit down long enough to work out their problems."

"That's hysterical Maggie! Kellie's brow furrowed. "You didn't really write that, did you?"

Kellie reached for the plate of cookies, but it was too far for her.

"I think that's clever Maggie," said Shirley, as she pushed the plate towards Kellie.

"Well, I also said that a mutual friend of both families could help them get along."

"Whew! I thought you would go into the merits of cotton and less starch," said Kellie.

"Oh I did, but the bulk of the essay was about finding someone, who wouldn't take sides."
Shirley flipped through the mail.

"Bills, more bills, trash, uh oh Kellie, it's the insurance company."

"Open it ma, oh wait I need to cross my fingers since I can't cross my toes." laughed Kellie. "Please God let the insurance company approve my prosthesis."

Shirley tore open the envelope. Her eyes scanned the letter while she mouthed the words silently.

"You're not smiling," said Maggie.

"Sigh, Kellie they turned you down because you are getting around with a wheelchair."

"What do they expect me to do hop around?"
Maggie laughed.

"Maggz it's not funny." Kellie's voice was breaking. "These people are morons. I've waited long enough. First, we had to wait until dad's insurance kicked in at the new job and now I'm waiting for someone with no IQ to decide if I need a leg."

"Sorry Kellie, I just laughed because I pictured you in a big furry bunny suit hopping on Pike Street." Maggie then looked down at her feet ashamed of her outburst.

Kellie's face was still red with anger. She burst into tears and almost rolled over Maggie's foot to get to the staircase. When she got there she stared at the steps. She left her crutches in her room since her dad carried her down this morning. At only 5'1" Kellie was more muscular than Maggie, but still tiny and easy to carry downstairs. It was only in a bathing suit that people could tell Kellie was the more athletically built twin. Maggie was just plain skinny.

Maggie peeked around from the dining room and saw Kellie looking hopelessly at the curved staircase.

"Hey, you need a lift?"

"Yeah, I need it, but I don't want it from you."

"Oh come on Kellie, I said I was sorry. You know I didn't mean to laugh. You're pissed at the insurance company and I would be too, but mom says they never give approval the first time you apply."

"That's right Kellie. We just have to send an appeal letter. Don't worry about it. Dad and I will make sure we send it in right away. Now do me a favor, let Maggie help you up the stairs, my back hurts from bending over patients in the dental chair today."

Kellie knew her mom was always in pain from being a dental hygienist. Her neck and back really suffered, but the hours were good. She worked 7 a.m. to 3 p.m., that's why she put up with it. She wanted to be home when the twins arrived from school.

Kellie blew a puff of air in frustration. When it hit her long bangs her hair looked like a curtain swaying in the breeze.

"Why don't I just run upstairs and get your stuff for you," said Maggie.

"No, I want to get my own stuff and do it myself," said Kellie.

Maggie didn't wait to be given the OK by Kellie she just stood in front of Kellie and put her arms around Kellie's rib cage. Kellie hugged Maggie's neck. When she was steady, Kellie grabbed the banister with her right hand as Maggie kept one arm around Kellie's back and reached up to hold Kellie's left hand over Maggie's shoulder. Then Maggie took a step and Kellie hopped up too.

At the top of the stairs, Kellie's crutches were propped against the wall at the entrance of her room. Her arms ached just looking at them. She hated using her crutches, but it was that or hop on one leg, which really never worked well. So she grabbed the crutches went into her room with its gray walls and black carpet. She sat down on the bed and thought about how last year it was so easy to get up the stairs before her accident. She used to love to jump two stairs at a time and slide down the banister in their old house up in Oneida. She missed that house, she missed her friends, but most of all she missed her right leg.

CHAPTER FIVE

MAGGIE I THINK I GOT SOMETHIN'
TO SAY TO YOU

Kellie finally wriggled her rear-end onto the bed and collapsed on the pillows.

She wondered why some people step in gold while other people step in crap-o-la? If this were Maggie, she would have gotten her fake leg and decorated it with an ankle bracelet and a snazzy shoe. Kellie believed life was easier for Maggie. She was the pretty twin after all. Before the accident, most people couldn't tell them apart especially, if they wore identical clothing and styled their hair the same way. But Kellie knew Maggie had more guys interested in her than she ever did. Their look was similar - they both had the same large bluish green eyes, high cheekbones and freckles, but Maggie's personality was the magnet that drew people in. Her broad smile made her more approachable. Whenever she walked she bounced as if a song was always playing in her head the whole time. She was also completely unaware of her beauty. Maggie constantly complained about her flat chest, freckled nose and bird-like legs. She told Kellie that she wanted Kellie's wavy hair. Kellie constantly ran her fingers through it and it always fell in place.

Kellie was more focused and rarely smiled without cause. A pity really because when she smiled her dimples showed. Her left one was deeper than the right and she had two small indentations on either side of her chin.

She grabbed her laptop from the nightstand next to her bed and logged on. With Maggie's nagging she finally got her profile on Buddybook. She only has three friends,

Maggie, Susan and Tara from back home. Maggie already has 150 friends. Maggie sent her one of those personality quizzes. Kellie left it blank for three days. Today, she decided to fill it out.

Getting to know you.
1. *Do you like blue cheese?* Yuck!
2. *What nicknames do you have?* Kell, Little Fishy (dad only). Wheelchair Girl and Tripod (two names I hate that kids in school call me).
3. *Have you ever ridden in an ambulance?* Yes, after my accident.
4. *Have you ever skipped school?* Not yet, but I hope to some day. It's hard not to be noticed in town when you're a kid in a wheelchair.
5. *Do you do push ups?* Yup, every time I fall trying to get in my wheelchair.
6. *What subject do you hate?* Math, anything with numbers makes my mind explode.
7. *What's your favorite sport?* Swimming, I used to be really good at it. Now, without the bottom part of my leg, I hope to get back my skills.
8. *What sport are you bad at?* Well, without a leg running isn't an option. Dancing doesn't look too promising either.
9. *Whose arms would you like to be in?* Kellie stared at the screen. Should she say it? Why not? Susan and Maggie already knew and Tara didn't know Eric anyway. Kellie compromised and just typed Eric's initials.
10. *What is your biggest dream?* To win the Paralympics in swimming.

The last one was her biggest wish, swimming meant freedom and going back to the old Kellie. She desperately wanted to be the old Kellie. Back then the flaws she thought she had like being flat chested, pale in comparison to losing the lower part of her leg.

She put her cursor over Maggie's profile picture. Maggie with her long blond, straight hair was holding their grey striped cat, Paisley. She was perfect. Kellie looked to the right corner of her screen. She had a friend request! When she clicked on it her excitement fell it was Sora Hayashi, an exchange student, who hangs out with Jade, the bully. She put her cursor over the choices "confirm" or "ignore". Should she give her a chance? It was a tough decision so Kellie decided to shut down the laptop and get ready to go out with Maggie.

People often mistook Maggie's warmth and friendliness for being shallow or flighty. Kellie knew better. Maggie wasn't a great student, but she could make something out of nothing. At a picnic, Kellie teased Maggie when she saw the red checked plastic table cloth.

"Hey Maggz, can you whip me up a down home dress out of this? It's so *pertie*!"

Kellie definitely had the textbook smarts, but Maggie was street smart and more creative. Maggie made daily trips to the Salvation Army store on Pike Street to buy used clothing each week. After ripping them a part, she makes something completely new out of them. Kellie once overheard Maggie tell Susan that the Salvation Army store and meeting Susan were the only two things that made the move to Port Jervis bearable.

Kellie knew she wasn't supposed to hear Maggie's conversation, but she felt bad because if it wasn't for her accident, the Joneses wouldn't have moved.

Kellie looked around her room with its gray walls and black furniture. In her bookcase were Jane Austen and Harry James classics alongside biographies of famous Olympians. Socks from last night were on the floor near the hamper. Her favorite red hoodie was tossed onto her rocking chair and notebooks were piled on haphazardly on her desk.

Maggie's bookcase is filled with fashion magazines and pattern books. They are all alphabetized and sorted according to year. Her closet is color coordinated and her mauve colored room is always spotless.

Kellie's room is always cluttered that is until Maggie sneaks in to clean it up. She worries about Kellie tripping over all her stuff, especially now.

"Hey!" Maggie came to the doorway interrupting Kellie's thoughts. "Are you ready to go to the creamery?"

"Do I have to be social?"

"Yes! Come on, I don't want to go by myself."

"You won't be by yourself. Susan is there."

"Yeah, but she'll be working." Maggie said as she picked up the socks and tossed them in the hamper. "She can't take more than one break and anyway she just got there." Maggie twirled her blond long hair into a bun and wound a ruffled ponytail holder around it. "She's going to be way too busy to sit around with me."

"All right let's roll."

"Are you going to wear that?" Maggie rolled her eyes looking at the faded blue sweatshirt Kellie was wearing.

"Uh, Yeah it's one of my favorites."

20

"It's old."

"I prefer to think it's broken in."

"Sigh! Just put on something else."

"Like what?"

"Wait here."

Maggie went back to her room and grabbed a cranberry button down shirt she made. She was saving it to wear to a movie night, but this was a fashion emergency.

"Here, put this on."

"Nice color. Is this a Maggie Mae design?"

"Yeah, I'm teaching myself to do princess seams. It used to be an old wrap around skirt from the 1970s. Can you imagine anyone wrapping their hips and thighs in that much cranberry fabric?"

"Not unless they wanted to look like one big, juicy berry!"

It was easier for Kellie to get down the stairs than going up. At their old house and before her accident, Kellie used to slide down the banister. Since the accident she is less of a dare devil.

"Ma, what do you think of Maggie's latest creation?"

"Sssh! Shut up. I don't need an argument now."

Too late.

"Oh Maggz, You didn't make that shirt. Come on, we saw it in H&M last week for $25. So how much do you have left from your babysitting money? You spent it all, didn't you?"

"No mom, I bought a skirt at the Salvation Army for $3 and took the buttons off of the old night shirt in the rag bin. I copied the shirt we saw at H&M."

Back in Oneida, Maggie became addicted to the show "Project Runway" and saved for six months to buy a

21

sewing machine. It's a used Singer. She saw it at a pawn shop for $75. She didn't dare ask for the money to buy it. Her father was unhappy with his job and money was tight so she baby-sat every kid in town until she saved enough to buy it.

"That's the seventh item of new clothing this week. You're supposed to save that money, not spend it."

"Mom, it's my money and I didn't spend it all. Why do you always give me a hard time?"

"I'm trying to teach you to save and you keep spending."

"Mom, I spent $20 out of the $140 I saved since March. Ever since I took a pack of pencils from the pharmacy when I was six, you've been on my back. Why can't you trust me?"

"I trust you. I just want to keep you on target, that's my job – I'm a parent."

"Here!" Maggie handed over the bank book.

"Why do you have these crazy stickers on your bank book?"

"It was a boring tan color. I wanted to jazz it up. It's my job – I'm a kid."

"Very funny," Shirley examined the bank book. It was all in order, Maggie even had the $20 grandma gave her for her birthday in addition to the babysitting money. She handed it back to Maggie.

"Good job Maggz."

"Now you believe me."

"I believe you more and more each day. To prove it, here's $10. Ice cream is on me."

"Sweet!" said Maggie.

"Thanks mom!" said Kellie.

"OK girls. Have fun and watch the traffic on Water Street."

Maggie and Kellie headed for the door. Shirley looked through the rest of the mail and felt bad for doubting Maggie.

"Hey Maggz!" said Shirley.

Maggie turned her head "Yeah?"

"You're getting pretty good with the sewing machine. I'm proud of you."

Her mom hadn't said anything like that in a long time.

"Thanks mom." Maggie smiled all the way to the creamery.

When Kellie's car accident happened, their parents decided to move so that everyone could have a fresh start. Their father got an offer on a good job and their mom found a dental hygienist job 10 minutes from Port Jervis so that she could be home when the twins finished their school day.

Maggie didn't complain when her parents told her they were leaving Oneida, but inwardly she was upset and angry. Life was just starting to bloom for Maggie.

No one but Susan knows this. The day Maggie's dad and mom told the twins that they were leaving Oneida in three weeks; Maggie got asked to the winter formal. She was really asked by three different guys. She refused all of them. They were football players not her type. When Ronnie asked she accepted immediately. He was her partner in chemistry lab. Well, technically, he did the work while Maggie watched. Ronnie is a nerd, but he has a quiet charm as Maggie discovered. When they were first paired up, Maggie was a little disappointed. Even though he was really smart, she thought he would treat her like a dumb blonde. She was sure they would have nothing in common.

To Ronnie, Maggie was just another person who hated chemistry. Ronnie took it upon himself, to show her the magic behind science. He is a tall, gangly kid with his own style, mixing plaids and stripes with Converse sneakers. Maggie respected that and told him that his outfits were unique and only something HE could get away with. Soon, they realized they had a lot more in common than they thought. Ronnie noticed Maggie sketching dresses during class, so he showed her how to do the labs through writing out the formulas and drawing pictures with each step. Finally, someone understood her. Maggie wasn't stupid; she was just a visual learner. Maggie in turn took him shopping and found a look that worked for him without offending the blind.

He called her "Magpie" because of her endless talking and she called him "Day Glow" because of his scary color combos. Ronnie finally asked Maggie to the formal. Well, kind of. What he actually said was "You're probably going to the formal with a football star, huh?"

"Nah, I was asked by three of them, but I don't want to be someone's arm candy. I was hoping to go with someone I could talk to."

Ronnie flipped his long black wedge of bangs out of his eyes and said, "We could hang out together at the dance if you want."

Maggie almost did a back flip, but she had to play it cool. "Yeah sure on one condition, I get to pick out your outfit, Day Glow."

"I wouldn't have it any other way, Magpie."

Four weeks later, after the move to Port Jervis, Maggie logged onto the computer and opened an email from Ronnie with a picture of himself in the outfit they picked out.

"Here's my GQ moment. Wish you were here to share it with me."

Maggie typed back. "You look perfect. I wish I was there too, but you'll have fun at the dance with Denise." Then she pressed "send". She knew that would be the last time she would hear from Ronnie. What would be the point? She was almost four hours away and about two years from a driver's license. Denise would probably steal his heart anyway.

"Why did Kellie have to get into that stupid car?" Maggie felt guilty for thinking that. How could she be so mean? There was nothing left she could do. So she threw herself on her bed, buried her face in her pillow and cried.

CHAPTER SIX

ERIC MAKES A MOVE

"Susie you make the best chocolate shake ever," said Eric sitting at the counter at the Riverside Creamery.

"It's a gift from the Gawds," Susan's Brooklyn accent was as thick as the hot fudge she poured over a sundae she was making for a 6-year-old boy. The little boy watched Susan with his tongue peeking out of his mouth, making sure she didn't skimp on the chocolate and forget the cherry.

Susan skated over to the edge of the counter with the Sundae. "Here ya go, kid." Then Susan turned to his mother. "That'll be $3.75 ma'am."

Susan rung her up at the register, took $4 and gave a quarter back with a smile and said. "Thanks and enjoy."

Mr. Reynolds peered at Susan from the kitchen. She was the best waitress he ever hired and not bad on roller skates either. Too bad Susan had such a tough life. She didn't talk much about it, but he heard the gossip around P.J. Other store owners told him about Susan's dad's death and her move from Brooklyn. Mr. Reynolds lost his wife to cancer three years ago so he understood her pain.

He overheard Susan talking to Maggie once about how she lied about her age to get a dry cleaning delivery job in Brooklyn because her dad was out of work for a few weeks and her family needed the money. After a trial run the owner hired her because she was so quick. Her secret was she skated to each customer's location. The owner never knew or else he would have flipped out.

Susan's mother, a pretty little thing with a Polish accent, was so kind. She made him batches of Chruschici cookies at Christmas. It was her way of thanking him for hiring Susan. Really, he thought he should thank her. At first, he hesitated when Susan came in to fill out an application. She was wearing a leather jacket with a T-shirt that said "Good Girl Gone Bad". How would she fit in at the Riverside Creamery? All the waitresses wore pink checkered shirts with hot pink poodle skirts and were required to roller skate in the ice cream parlor modeled after a 1950s diner. It turns out Susan, lied about her age to get a dry cleaning delivery job. The owner never knew that Susan was so fast with deliveries because she skated to each customer's location.

When Susan spoke, each word was punctuated with a Brooklyn burst of tough. Folks here wouldn't respond well to that. In fact, George, who owned the hardware store across the street, predicted she would steal from him in a matter of days. Mr. Reynolds ignored the advice. He knew she needed a chance. On her first day, when the streets were flooded after a torrential rain, she came in a half hour early soaked to the skin. He knew then Susan was a good, reliable kid and he was right.

"Maggz, I can do it, let go." Kellie stubbornly opened the door to the parlor and rested it on her back wheel as she slid through. Maggie rolled her eyes letting Kellie take the lead towards a table by the window.

"Hey Maggz, Kell, what can I whip up for ya," Susan said as she glided across the room and did a half turn at the table. She took the pencil from behind her ear and flipped over a page on her guest check pad.

"I'll have a hot fudge brownie sundae heavy on the fudge please."

"What about you Kell, the usual?" Susan started writing down two scoops of mint chocolate chip when Kellie looked up at the counter and saw Eric.

"Uh, I'll get the fruit cup, please."

"Are you nuts?" said Susan. "Nobody orders fruit here, except Mrs. Connolly. In fact, I don't even think we have any that isn't swimming in heavy syrup anyway. Hey, Mr. Reynolds, this one wants fruit. Should I run to the supermarket?"

"That's the funniest thing I've heard all day, kid," said Mr. Reynolds.

Kellie put her finger to her mouth. "Ssh he'll hear you."

"Who, old man Reynolds?" said Susan.

"No him!" Kellie's head moved in the direction of the ice cream counter.

Susan looked back at Eric who was blowing bubbles in his shake. What a doofus, she thought. Kellie's taste certainly wasn't hers.

"Please, he's drinking away 500 calories. Do you think he cares if someone else eats a lousy 300? So what are ya really havin'?" said Susan.

"Um, well I have to start swim training tomorrow." Kellie began looking at the sherbet flavors.

"Hey, why don't you share my sundae? I don't want it all to go to my hips anyway. Mom gave us the money so then we will give a bigger tip to Susan," said Maggie.

"Hey, I love that idea," grinned Susan.

"Okay, and I'll have a diet soda too," said Kellie, knowing she would stick to the soda until Eric left.

"Gawd! What we girls do for guys," said Susan as she took their menus and skated back into the kitchen.

"She's right you know. Who cares what he thinks?" said Maggie as she searched for change in her purse for the jukebox. She loved the old 50s tunes even though if any kid at school asked she would tell them "Good Charlotte" was her favorite. So in a way Maggie also cared what others thought about her too.

Susan came back with the diet soda and shook her head. "There she goes again."

"Who?" said the twins at the same time.

Mary-Chris Murphy, the new waitress. Susan nodded in the direction of a tall, thin, teenager with red long curly hair and lots of freckles. She was pretty in a Raggedy Ann, sweet and innocent way. As Mary-Chris selected an ice cream dish she appeared to float from task to task like Tinkerbell. Then it happened: Mary-Chris crossed herself and began to talk softly to no one in particular over several scoops of chocolate ice cream on top of a brownie before gliding through the room. Susan's eyes followed her as Mary-Chris dragged her purple stopper on her right skate to stop at the table and in a graceful swoop put the Sundae in front of the customer.

"Was she just praying over the ice cream?" said Kellie.

"Yup" said Susan. "I didn't think God had time to worry about ice cream when there are so many other problems in the world. You would think the war in Iraq would keep him busy enough."

Maggie shrugged her shoulders. "So she's a little religious."

"Ya think? Susan laughed. "She just said a prayer over a Sundae because it's called Devil's Food Brownie Bomb."

"Can you imagine what she will do when she serves a "Death By Chocolate shake?" said Kellie a little too loudly. Several people turned around towards their table.

"Come on Kellie, don't be so judgmental." whispered Maggie. "She's probably really nice."

Susan's eyes rolled. "Oh, she's an angel."

"Careful, she may substitute the Devil's food cake for Angel Food and really piss off the chocolate lovers." Maggie shot Kellie a dirty look.

"Does she go to Port Jervis High School? I've never seen her before and she looks like she's our age," said Maggie.

"No, she goes to Trinity Catholic School and lives five minutes from here just over the bridge in Pennsylvania.

"I think I'll call her "M.C." for Master Catholic in da house." Kellie said.

"It can be her new rap name," Susan laughed.

"Kell, don't you dare, you'll embarrass us." Maggie said "Shh, she's coming over."

"Mary-Chris, I want you to meet my friends, Kellie and Maggie Jones. They're new here, but they're my friends, so you'll see them around a lot."

"Hi, are you sisters or cousins?"

"Twins," Kellie and Maggie grinned when they replied at the same time.

"I wish I had a twin. I just have a pesky little brother, Joseph."

"Mary-Chris, that's an unusual, but pretty name," said Maggie.

"Thanks. It's a lot to live up to. My mother named me for the Virgin Mary and Jesus Christ. My brother is named for Joseph. Our dog is Bethlehem and our fish is

Baby Jesus. Most people think it's a little weird that we're such devout Catholics."

"Well, my mom named me after a dumb Rod Stewart song, "Maggie Mae". My mom had a thing for musicians. Kellie's middle name is "Davy" after "Davy Jones" the lead singer from that 60s band "The Monkees"."

"Do you have any pets?" said Mary-Chris.

"We have a cat." said Maggie. "Her name is Paisley. I named her after my favorite pattern. I'm kind of a fashionista."

"Kind of?" said Kellie. Maggie stuck her tongue out.

"I have a cat," volunteered Susan. "But I can't tell you his name."

"Why?" said Mary-Chris to an audience of giggles.

"Well, because you will want me to go to confession and that's not my thing."

"Oh come on, it can't be that bad," said Mary-Chris.

"Okay". Susan hesitated. "His name is Satan."

In an effort to fit in, Mary-Chris laughed uncomfortably as she made the sign of the cross. "Poor kitty! I'll have to pray for him," then she said goodbye and moved towards the counter.

"You do that Mary-Chris, and at the same time, tell God to stop him from clawing the furniture," said Susan. Maggie saw Mary-Chris try to hide her red face as she filled the straw containers. Maggie took some money out of her purse and got up to go towards the jukebox nearby. "Susan seems tough, but she's really a good friend. Don't worry, she's just teasing you."

"Oh, I know, but it's hard because most kids hate to go to church. They don't understand why I look forward to it." Mary-Chris took a wet rag from her apron pocket and wiped down the table.

Maggie folded her arms over her chest. "Who cares what people think? My sister has learned the hard way to block out what others think of her. It isn't easy, but it's something I have also learned to deal with."

"Do you mind if I ask what happened to your sister?"

"No not at all. She lost her leg in a car accident last year. We're new to the area so the kids around here don't know that she wasn't born this way. In fact, she's hoping to get a prosthetic leg soon and train for the Paralympics."

"What's the Paralympics?"

"It's an Olympics set up for physically challenged people."

"How did she find out about that?"

"Her aide, Mrs. Connolly told her about it and found this coach, who she is going to meet tomorrow."

"Wow, that's really cool. I admire her," said Mary-Chris.

"So do I." said Maggie. "It was nice meeting you." Then Maggie slipped the quarters into the jukebox selected a song and joined Susan, who was now over at the ice cream counter.

Kellie took out a book from her purse and pretended to read just in case Eric looked her way. Out of the corner of her eye she saw him get up and walk towards her. "Oh no," she groaned.

"Hey, mind if I sit here?" Before Kellie could say anything Eric pulled out the chair and sat down.

"I guess not," said Kellie sarcastically. She was really happy and nervous about it, but she tried to make it look like she didn't care.

"So, whatcha doin' this summer?" Eric said while fiddling with straws in the old fashioned pop up glass canister.

"Just swimming at Delaware Valley High and helping out at the Port Jervis library." said Kellie.

"You swim?" said Eric.

"Well, yeah, and I'm good at it too," bragged Kellie. "I'm starting tomorrow with a new coach named Eileen Foley. She's going to get me ready for the Paralympics next year."

"The Para what?" Eric looked puzzled.

"The Paralympics. It's like the Olympics for the disabled."

"Wow, that's pretty cool. You know I'll probably be there when you train. I'm doing a soccer clinic for kids this summer at DV. It starts tomorrow at 10 a.m."

"Yeah, I'll be there until 1 p.m., marinating in chlorine," Kellie shocked herself that she could still be funny and nervous at the same time.

"Are you doing anything after 1 p.m.?" said Eric,

"I'll probably be ready to eat someone's arm off by then." The sarcasm fell out of Kellie's mouth before she could take it back. Stupid...he isn't supposed to know about her huge appetite.

"Great! Maybe we'll go for a slice." The offer fell out of Eric's mouth before he thought about it too. Jade, his girlfriend wouldn't like it.

"What about Jade?" Kellie said it, but was so ticked at herself for it. Who cares about that piece of toxic waste; he asked YOU out dummy.

"Well, it's not a date. Just a buddy thing, ya know?" said Eric. "One athlete to another." He didn't want her to think he would cheat on Jade even though Jade cheated on him plenty of times.

"Oh sure, no problem, sounds good." As soon as Kellie said it, she had a stabbing pain in her stomach. She felt the same way when she did a belly flop after diving into the deep end of the pool.

CHAPTER SEVEN

FORGIVENESS

Kellie turned on the computer searched to see if Tara, her closest friend up in Oneida was logged on. Tara left six messages on her voice mail and countless e-mails. Kellie didn't know what to say, so she never replied until now since she thought the distance between them was much more than geography.

She began typing. "Hey Tara, it's Kell."

"Kellie! Oh my God, I'm so glad you IM'd. Uh, how's it goin' in Railroadville?"

"Port Jervis is OK, I guess." after typing Kellie leaned her head on her right hand.

"That doesn't seem all that great." said Tara. There was a long pause in between before Tara typed again desperate to continue the conversation. "How was the last day of school for you?"

"It's good I guess. Maggz and I just came home from the ice cream parlor," said Kellie running her fingers through a wave in her hair. It reminded her she had to use the flat iron again. Maggie had perfectly straight blond hair. Just shampoo and go. Kellie got knots in her hair if someone breathed on it.

"I'm glad you're writing to me. I was worried when you didn't return my calls or emails." Tara's eyes were tearing up. "I miss you."

Back in Oneida neighbors joked that Tara was Kellie's real twin and not Maggie. They had so much fun running down to the docks to feed the ducks or going to the boardwalk in the summer to gorge on cotton candy and

35

then jump onto a ride called "The Cobra". They used to bet on which one of them would get sick the fastest.

"That ice cream parlor sounds like a lot of fun." Tara typed quickly, but tried sound positive.

Kellie knew why the conversation with Tara felt strange. She just hoped the feeling would go away and they could get back to normal one day. But guilt can seep into you like a red stain on a white shirt.

Last winter, Tara told Kellie to get into a car driven by Tara's cousin, Dean. Dean drank beer before picking them up. Tara smelled it on his breath. In fact, Tara saw one beer can in between the seats. They didn't have another ride home from the party. Tara figured at 19, Dean was an experienced driver. He could handle it. Tara was afraid, but she didn't want to cause any drama in front of the other kids. Both girls couldn't call home because they snuck out to go to the party, but they didn't want to walk home in the snow.

"Tara, are you still there?" Kellie thought she might have logged off.

"Yup, I'm still here. But I gotta go," Tara said quickly.

"Wait, we never talk about it. I think we should. You know I don't blame you..." before Kellie could finish, Tara interrupted.

"You should. It's my fault."

"Excuse me, did you drink the beer?" Kellie asked.

"No, but I saw the empty can. I never told you that. I saw it tucked between the seats. And..." Tara couldn't finish the sentence.

"And I still made the decision to get into the car," said Kellie.

"Yes, but you didn't know about the beer," said Tara.

"I smelled it when Dean was yelling at us to get in and close the door. And I also saw that he was driving a little crazy. I could have gotten out of the car then, but I was afraid to embarrass you." Kellie stared at her stump where her calf and foot used to be and rubbed the bottom of it. "Anyway, when the cops came and gave him a breathalyzer it wasn't beyond the legal limit. It was the cell phone that he dropped. That's what made him skid. It was an accident and no one else got hurt."

"You did. You're in a wheelchair!" said Tara.

"Really, is that what those wheels are for?" said Kellie.

"Stop it. It's not funny. I should have insisted that we walk or at the very least told him to slow down and stay off the phone," Tara yelled.

"So you're his guardian angel now?" Kellie yelled. "Look, I can't say I wasn't totally ticked off at you in the beginning. I was, but the shrink my parents paid big money for said the blame isn't yours. It's Dean's. The shrink cost enough so I believe her. She also says I'm to blame."

"Why are you to blame? You're the victim."

"No, I could have made a different decision. What do they say, 'Every man for himself?'"

"Every PERSON for his or herself," said Tara. They both laughed. There it was a glimmer of the free spirited, self righteous, always ready for a cause Tara.

"Look, the health insurance morons turned me down for the prosthesis. My parents are sending an appeal letter. I really can't believe they have to. I mean, it's pretty obvious that I need one. But who knows what they'll

37

decide. Hopefully, soon they will piece me back together like a broken Barbie doll." Kellie laughed remembering how her father was always fixing Barbie when she was little. Those long legs seemed to pop off so easily.

"Since you're getting a Barbie makeover, do you think you can put me down for a boob job too?" laughed Tara.

"Hey, you can only get one tune up per customer. Besides, if the insurance people are handing out boobs, I'm cutting you in line. You don't need them as much as I do." Kellie looked down and remembered her mom saying that she didn't fully blossom until she turned 18. So it would be four more years to go before she reached Pamela Anderson status. That wasn't going to be easy since right now she looked more like her father from the waist up than her mother. Tara laughed realizing that Kellie was right.

Kellie heard her dad shouting from downstairs. "Kellie, supper is on the table."

"Damn, my dad is calling me to dinner. Hang on." Kellie stopped typing. "I'll be there in a minute dad," she shouted.

"Anyway, Eric doesn't care if I'm flat-chested."

"Who's Eric?"

"The star soccer player at P.J. High he asked me out today."

"Ooh tell me more. What does he look like?"

"He's tall, with reddish blond hair and seems to like me so he's blind."

"What? Come on."

"Well, he has to be. He asked me instead of Maggie."

"Kellie, stop it. It sounds like this guy has good taste since he's dating my best friend."

Kellie's dad shouted again. "Kellie Davy Jones, children are starving all over the world and would give their arm for one of your mother's meals. Come on before it gets cold."

"I really have to go now Tara, I'll e-mail you Sunday and let you know how the date went."

"Yeah OK, I should go too. Talk to you soon."

After she logged off her e-mail, Tara took a deep breath. As she exhaled she felt some of the guilt leave with it. Only some of it though. The rest she kept tucked in her brain as a lesson. She sat down at her computer, logged onto the Internet and typed the word "peer pressure" and pressed "go". Six hundred and eighty seven thousand hits popped up. That's when she realized, she wasn't alone.

CHAPTER EIGHT

JADE'S RISE TO QUEEN OF P.J. HIGH

Don't ask Jade Santiago how she got so popular. It's a mystery to her too. It certainly wasn't due to her charming personality. She isn't a kind person. Of course, kids learn how to be kind from the way a person is treated by others. Jade's example was gone by her fourth birthday. Jade's mother, Carla, died of cancer and she was left in her father's care. Carla was beautiful. Tall and thin with big green eyes. Jade looks just like her. Green eyes are unusual for Puerto Ricans - but not unheard of. Jade was named for her beautiful emerald green eyes. Carla loved Jade and since she was her only child, she spoiled her. For Jade, Carla's face has faded over the years, but the sound of her sweet voice singing her to sleep in Spanish is a sound Jade will never forget. Alone at night, she tries to conger up the soft melodious tone of her mother's voice.

Jade's father, Delwood Santiago known as "Del" by his drinking buddies, was gentle when he was sober. Unfortunately, Jade rarely saw that side of him since he started drinking heavily the day after her mom's funeral. By the time she was 6 Jade was hiding wine and beer bottles in the house. Anyone from the outside would think she was playing a game, but Jade knew those bottles led to angry shouts, cursing, and eventually she would get hit after he held a bottle in his hand for too long. As she got older she realized the bottles weren't the cause of her father's rage, it was the liquid inside them. So early one Saturday morning an 8-year-old Jade, poured each one down the drain.

Her father ambled into the kitchen just as Jade poured the last bottle of red wine down the stark white sink. Del swung his open hand around and smacked the bottle out of Jade's hand. The bottle crashed against the corner of the sink and a broken piece of glass flew up cutting Jade along her right cheek. The blood droplets fell and mixed in with the wine stained basin.

Del called an ambulance. They sat in the hospital emergency room with Jade holding gauze to her face while Del crafted an explanation to the doctors. One of many countless tales he would tell.

Jade still remembers her father telling the stern looking doctor, "My daughter loves her peanut butter and jelly sandwiches. She couldn't wait for me to come and get the jelly from the top shelf. You know kids. She decided to climb up onto the counter and get it herself. Well, she dropped the jar and a piece of glass caught her in the face. I don't know what I'm gonna do with this little girl."

Five stitches later, a frightened Jade walked home with her father from the hospital. They stopped at the liquor store and he bought two more bottles of wine and a six pack of beer.

"Here!" he said as he shoved a brown bag into her arms. "Don't you dare drop these. Do you know how much these cost? Girl, don't you ever touch your papa's stuff again, you hear?"

That's when Jade knew that her father loved his booze more than he could ever love her. There were more trips to the hospital. Many would be blamed on her clumsy pre-teen adventures. Most of her injuries were caused by Dell, others she caused herself. That's what happens when you get tipsy. Jade started drinking at age 9. She wanted her father to share something with her. Oddly enough she thought the alcohol gave her courage.

By the time, she was 13, Jade was drinking regularly and her mood swings were evident. People in town suspected something was wrong. They whispered behind her back, but they never offered help and no one dared to investigate. Del and Jade were intimidating to people. Del was a giant at six foot five. His biceps were each the size of a women's waist. Jade got her strong jaw from her father and as pretty as her eyes were, they weren't gentle like her moms. There was anger behind her stare.

One more fact kept residents quiet. Del's brother, Jorge is Chief of Police. Jorge is a good man, but he spent his life defending his little brother. Jorge believed that Del was doing his best he could and people just didn't understand his brother's hardships. Jorge tried to help with money and food, especially when Del had to sell his home and move into the trailer park. Del said he lost his job because his boss wanted him to work evenings. He refused because he had to be home for Jade.

The real reason was, Del overslept so many times that the boss fired him. Jorge didn't know this. He didn't check. He trusted his brother's story. Funny thing is, Jorge checked out people's stories for a living. He was really careful with his work and the people he dealt with except when it came to family. Jorge wanted to believe him and so he did.

Jorge and his wife, Joya, have five kids of their own to look after. They didn't have the time to pry into Del and Jade's life. They didn't know Del had to rent the trailer because he drank away his mortgage money or that he regularly took his anger out on Jade. Jade knew why her

42

dad was in debt and resented her alcoholic father for making her live in a trailer and being his punching bag.

Gradually, she grew to hate everyone who was happy. Sometimes jealous anger just swallowed her whole like a rash overtaking her body. She could feel it rise and there was no way to stop it.

CHAPTER NINE

CHANGE IS GOOD

After dinner, Maggie and Kellie sat outside on the rambling front porch. At least, Kellie sat there. Maggie bounced around from sitting to doing cartwheels on the lawn. Kellie balanced her laptop trying to keep the Internet single from inside the house.

"Woo Hoo!" Eric asked me to be his buddy on Buddybook. Kellie's heart started beating fast. "What should I do?"

"Ooh that's a good sign. Press the "confirm" button, you dope!"

Kellie, pressed it forgetting to delete the "Getting To Know You" survey from her profile.

"So Eric asked you out?" said Maggie as she jumped up to hit a high branch on a crab apple tree. "Damn, I can never get that branch." said Maggie. "If only I'd grow a few more inches."

"Don't look at me. I can't get it for you." Kellie laughed. It was a little painful to say it, but it was a true.

Maggie leaped in front of Kellie's wheelchair. "Never mind, tell me exactly what he said?"

"Nothin'" Kellie shrugged. "It didn't look like nothing. You have to tell me. It's a twin thing."

Back at Riverside Creamery after Maggie selected her song at the jukebox, she went over to the counter to talk to Susan. After they chatted awhile, Maggie swung around on the stool and saw Eric talking to Kellie. Maggie stayed back observing. It seemed that Kellie was playing it cool, shrugging her shoulders and talking briefly. In the other chair, Eric was trying to impress. He was fidgeting

44

with his straw and had one leg sticking out from the table ready for a getaway. Maggie debated whether she should stay on the stool or not. But she didn't need to worry. Within a matter of minutes, she heard Eric say "see ya tomorrow" and he was out the door. Tomorrow was Saturday so when would Eric and Kellie see each other unless it WAS a date.

"Come on, I heard him tell you that he would see you tomorrow." Maggie held Kellie's gaze.

Kellie looked at the ground. "We might grab pizza after my swim practice and after he finishes coaching the little kids in soccer. It's no biggie."

"No biggie! This is HUGE!" Maggie said. "My sister is dating the king of Port Jervis High School. "The Sultan of Soccer". We have to go to the mall, that's all there is to it. We have to get an outfit for your pizza date...or maybe you can wear something I have."

"What's wrong with my clothes?"

"Let's not spoil the night, shall we?" She and Kellie looked alike, but they never had the same taste in clothes. Maggie was more into Charlotte Russe, Rave, and funky junior styles. Kellie preferred jeans with golf shirts and rainbow belts. More like cheap J. Crew.

"It's not a date. It's just a buddy thing. That's what he said."

"It didn't seem like a buddy thing from where I was sittin'." Maggie leaped over a sewer cover. She never walked on them for fear she would fall in. She knew it was dumb, but it was just one of her quirks.

"You saw us?"

"Of course, I was sitting on the stool tryin' to give you some space. Nice moves. You played it cool. You go girl!" Maggie lightly punched Kellie in the arm.

"Stop with the 'you go girl' stuff. Do you think I looked okay?" Kellie never felt good enough with the exception of swimming. Of course, that was the one thing Maggie couldn't do better. In fact, Maggie never swam at all. She has been terrified of water since she almost drowned in a lake when she was six. Except for baths and showers she never went in the water. In fact, if given the choice, she preferred showers.

"You were great, very breezy and very cool. But I thought you didn't care," said Maggie

"I didn't say I didn't care. I just don't know why he would be interested," said Kellie, pointing to her stump.

"Come on, get over it. You're great with two legs or one. Hey, maybe he figures if he gets out of line he only has to worry about one leg kicking him? Unlike Jade, she's got both legs and if she kicks him with those big feet his soccer career is over with."

Just then their neighbor, Mr. Cohen, walked across the street to their mailbox. "Hi girls, we got this by mistake. Do you want me to bring it over to you?"

"Nah, that's OK," said Kellie. "Could just pop it in the box, please?"

"OK, no problem."

"Thanks, Mr. Cohen."

Maggie scrunched up her forehead. Kellie knew Maggie only did this when she was worried. Jade could be crazy jealous and she already saw her take her anger out on Kellie.

"You know, maybe he'll have to worry about two legs soon," said Maggie. "Race you to the mailbox. Maybe the insurance approval is there today."

"Maggie it can't be there, they just rejected me a few hours ago."

46

"Maybe they changed their mind," said Maggie as she grabbed the handles of Kellie's wheelchair.

"Maggz, I know you're the optimistic one, but this is impossible."

"Positive thinking my twincess, I shall push your chariot to the mailbox."

Maggie and Kellie got to the white mailbox and Maggie opened it peering inside.

"Nothin, just a post card from Aunt Linda," said Maggie.

"Let me see that. Is she somewhere tropical?"

Aunt Linda, their mother's sister loved to travel. She always sent a postcard to the twins and Maggie always framed them like art.

"Ooh, Bora Bora"

"Where's that?" asked Kellie.

"I don't know, but it definitely doesn't look boring, boring."

They both laughed. Maggie pushed Kellie's wheelchair back onto the driveway. When they got to the porch, Maggie struggled to give that first push up the ramp.

Kellie could feel Maggie's struggle and was mad she couldn't get herself up the ramp.

"Maggz, I still don't understand why I was rejected in the first place? I was in a car accident. They amputated my leg below the knee. How hard is this to understand? Maybe she could use prosthesis, ya think?"

"Kell, it's only a matter of time. Don't worry, it will happen." Maggie got Kellie up to the top of the ramp and wheeled her around to the front of the white Victorian with navy blue shudders.

"What if those morons reject me again?" What if they won't cover it?" Kellie was scared she would have to sit in a wheelchair her whole life. It frightened her almost as much as learning to walk all over again.

"They won't reject you, again. Come on, let's go inside. It's starting to get buggy out here."

CHAPTER TEN

A NEW DAY

"Wake up, little fishy." Kellie's father's voice was gravely and low. She never needed an alarm clock with him around. "It's time to get up so mom can bring you to swim lessons."

Kellie hugged her pillow. "I'm so tired."

"Come on; get up before I bring out the heavy artillery." Harold was known to get his trumpet out and play - really badly - until the kids got out of bed.

"OK, OK." Kellie sat up and her dad gave her the pink robe hanging on the door. She put her arms in the sleeves and he helped position the wheelchair so that she could scoot her butt into it. It was 7 a.m., and she had to be at the pool at 8:30. She showered and changed into her suit with her mother's help. She then started blow drying her hair, laughing since it was going to be wet in an hour. A girl's got to look good just in case.

She threw a cute pink velvet jogging outfit into her tan gym bag. The BeBe outfit was Maggie's and she insisted that Kellie wear it to eat pizza with Eric. Maggie found the outfit for five dollars at the Salvation Army on Pike Street. It was brand new with the tags still on it. It's amazing what people toss out. But if they do, Maggie will find it.

Kellie wasn't even sure Eric would remember the date since he asked so nonchalantly. And what was she going to do with her mother? Her mom would have to drive her to the pizza place. Oh man, she didn't think about that. What if mom said no? What if her mother sat with them! A look of panic came over Kellie's face.

"Geez, I just came in to get some lotion," said Maggie looking at Kellie. Kellie turned off the hair dryer and closed the door telling Maggie about her dilemma with mom.

"Well, why didn't you tell her?" Maggie said brushing her perfectly straight blond hair.

"I forgot." Kellie said.

"But you didn't forget to put it on your Buddybook status." Maggie smiled. "Going to eat a slice with E.G." Kellie looked shocked that Maggie saw her status so soon after she wrote it.

"Don't worry, she won't mind. She'll just go food shopping. You know, the grocery store is her favorite place. It's like her natural habitat." said Maggie.

"Maybe you're right, but I didn't want to make a big deal of it."

"Girl, until we start driving, we've got no choice," Maggie said grabbing a tube of lotion out of the medicine cabinet.

Kellie talked to her mom and surprisingly she wasn't bothered by the extra time it would take to drop her off at the pizza place and pick her up later. She seemed thrilled that someone other than Maggie and Susan was spending time with Kellie. Shirley told Aunt Linda once that high school can be the worst experience. Throw in Kellie's challenges and it can be a disaster.

Shirley, Kellie and Maggie got into the car. They dropped off Maggie at her first job at the Book Nook on Front Street and then headed to Delaware Valley High School five minutes over the bridge that connects New York to Pennsylvania.

Kellie was a little nervous. Why does everything have to happen in one day? She thought to herself. First, I have to deal with a new coach and then I have to meet Eric. And what if he forgets?

As soon as they got to the school, Kellie and her mom went into the locker room to drop off her gym bag. Then Kellie did some arm stretches. Kellie reached for her mother's shoulders and wrapped her right arm around them like she was her buddy. Shirley supported Kellie by holding onto her waist as Kellie hopped to the pool side.

Coach Eileen Foley was already swimming in the pool. When she saw Kellie she swam to the ladder and climbed out.

"Can I help you out?" Mrs. Foley put her hand out. "I'd shake your hands but you look a little busy." When Eileen said it she realized it could be taken in the wrong way. But instead both Kellie and Shirley laughed.

"Well, you're right about that. I'm Shirley Jones and before you ask, no, I'm not going to sing with the Partridge Family today." Referring to the 70s television show, which starred Shirley Jones as the mother of the musical family.

"I would hope not. Boy, they really stunk didn't they?" Eileen, a pretty lady in her 30s with dark hair and porcelain skin laughed with Shirley.

However, Kellie was in the dark about the whole Partridge thing. "Were they a bunch of birds that sang or something?"

"No, I guess we're showing our age here. It was a dumb TV show in the 70s. Anyway, I hear you are a strong swimmer with a goal to compete in the Paralympics. There are a few competitions we will need to get ready for in order to qualify. Before I say I'm behind you on this, I need to see what you've got so dive in and let me look at your technique."

"I'm not sure how I'm going to do." Kellie said with a quiver in her voice. "I used to swim competitively when I had both legs and I came in first place a lot. But since the car accident, I haven't even dipped my toe in the pool. I'm not sure if I can dive in."

Eileen reached for the bottle of water on the bench. "Well, I guess you need to just jump in and try it. Just remember you can take the failure, but the failure can't take you. Let's get you over to the ladder at the far end of the pool and practice balance and diving first. Take your hand and grab onto the ladder to balance on the side that you have your stump on. Now, squeeze your butt muscles in and your tummy. Breathe in and put your other arm out and let go of the ladder. You have to rely on the middle of your body to keep you standing."

Eileen stood beside her as Kellie stood on her own. Kellie couldn't believe it.

"OK, now grab onto the ladder again and breathe before you turn blue." laughed Eileen. "Think about the form that you used to have when approaching a dive; bringing your arms up over your head and springing off your feet, correct? Now, balance yourself again and when you are ready swing your arms overhead and spring off the pool side."

Kellie did this and at first she grabbed the ladder again. Eileen saw this and repeated. "You can take the failure, but the failure can't take you. Let go of the ladder, bring your arms up overhead and go for it."

Kellie listened to the coach's instructions, took a deep breath and dove in. The heated water calmed the sting on her side. She went down to the bottom and used her arms to push her back up to the surface. A loud roar of clapping and hooting greeted her.

Shirley stood up and shouted in the bleachers "Go Kellie!"

"Ma, stop it. You're embarrassing me." But she wasn't really that upset. She was relieved. The first jump into the deep end was done.

Then she heard a hoot that echoed off the walls. "Yay, Kellie!"

She looked up and it was Eric standing by the door. Her heart began to pound. The first jump was over, but a bigger leap was needed to get her over the next obstacle.

CHAPTER ELEVEN

A SLICE OF ADVICE

Kellie decided to play off Eric's loud applause by clowning around. She waved to the crowd of three and said "Thank you, thank you. Now where's my gold medal?"

"In time, Miss Risk, in time," Eileen smiled.

"What did you call me?" Kellie wasn't sure what her coach said.

"Miss Risk as in"risk taker". I give nicknames to all my athletes. You're willing to take the risk and that's the first step to victory. Now, since you're already in the pool, how about doing a breaststroke. One lap, I just want to see your form and how fast you can go with the bottom part of your leg missing."

Kellie let go of the bottom of the ladder and faced the opposite end of the pool.

"Ready... Set...Go!" Coach Eileen pressed the time clock.

Kellie bent her right leg and pushed off against the wall kicking her leg and her stump she tried to propel herself as fast as possible while moving her arms like a bent windmill. She felt off balance without the leg. It was tough keeping her balance as she turned to the side for a breath. She knew her speed had declined, but she felt so free in the water. No chair, no one lifting her or repositioning her. She was in control with just the heated water trickling off her finger tips each time she raised her arms back and out of the water. Why did she rob herself of this experience for so long?

Eric was done with his soccer clinic for the day. So he decided to sit down on the bleachers and watch. He saw a lady sitting in the front with light hair and so he moved towards her.

"Hi, I'm Eric Green, Kellie's friend."

"Eric, nice to meet you, I'm Kellie's mom."

"Oh, hi, you look just like Kellie and Maggie."

"Well, I guess they look more like me since I was here before them." Eric turned red and Mrs. Jones felt bad for correcting him.

"So how do you know Kellie?" Mrs. Jones was curious. She only heard about the kid this morning when Kellie told her about the pizza date. Kellie never talked about friends anyway unless it was Susan or Tara. She knew making friends was tough for Kellie now and she didn't want to push her. But she did worry about her. It wasn't easy having an aide around all the time even though Mrs. Connolly was a blessing.

"I met her and Maggie at school. Kellie was in my study hall class and Maggie had the same lunchtime.

"I'm a year older than the twins, but Kellie always helped me with social studies. I'm not that good at remembering dates."

"Hmm...he's also not that good at calling a date, a date. A buddy thing! Who does he think he's kidding?" thought Mrs. Jones.

"I'm teaching soccer to the little kids over the summer here."

"Are you on the PJ soccer team?" Mrs. Jones didn't know the first thing about soccer or any other sport except swimming.

"I'm the star player." Eric knew he was bragging, but it was the one thing he felt successful at according to his dad.

"Well, that's great. Kellie loved soccer, she used to play, ya know?"

"How?" This was news to Eric. He didn't know of any teams for disabled kids.

"Before the accident last winter, she had both her legs. She was quite the athlete. She played on the Junior Varsity soccer team in Oneida. She was their top swimmer on the girls' team too."

"What about Maggie?" Eric just asked the question, but he really had no interest in Maggie. He just figured they were twins so they probably played together.

"Oh no, Maggie's sport is shopping. The twins look alike, but they're definitely two different people. And I kind of like it that way. They both have great qualities, but are independent kids." Mrs. Jones said this without taking her eyes off the pool.

"Kellie never told you she played sports?" said Mrs. Jones.

"No, I always thought she was born without her leg."

"Well, no and that's why I felt bad that she gave up so much. It was more than losing her leg; she seemed to lose sight of her future and stopped doing everything. It wasn't until she came across the Paralympics web site that she got interested in swimming again. These private lessons will cost a fortune, but my husband and I will do anything to get Kellie interested in life again."

"Wow, I never knew. I guess I don't know her that well. I was hoping to grab a pizza afterwards with her.

Would you like to come too?" Eric figured he would earn some brownie points with the mom. What the heck.

"Thank you. That's very sweet of you, but I have to do some grocery shopping after this." She watched his face relax and waited a minute before adding "But I can drop both of you off at the pizza parlor and then take you home in two hours."

"I can take Kellie if you want. I'm a good driver. I got my license three months after getting the permit. I passed on the first try."

"Thanks for the offer, Eric, but Kellie has her wheelchair and she is hesitant to get into cars since the accident. See, she got into a car after a party in Oneida. The driver dropped his cell phone and crashed the car. That's how Kellie lost her leg."

"I understand." Eric didn't want to push his luck. "I guess it's best if I meet you there. Is it okay if you drop her off at 2 p.m. at the pizza place on Front Street in Port Jervis?"

"That's fine." said Mrs. Jones.

"I can walk, well, roll Kellie home if you like." Eric laughed a little and then realized his comment could have been taken the wrong way.

But Mrs. Jones laughed too, which relaxed Eric. "No, I have to swing by there anyway so I'll pick her up on my way back."

Mrs. Jones sat with a worried look on her face. Eric seemed like a nice kid. She looked up at Kellie, who was diving off the side of the pool perfectly in just this short amount of time. The muscles in her arms tensed as she made her way across the pool again in a robotic motion. Perhaps Kellie was stronger than she gave her credit for.

Mrs. Jones scolded herself for being so protective, but she didn't really want her daughter to be "walked" home just yet. Kellie couldn't fight back if he put moves on her. And then Mrs. Jones laughed to herself. Kellie could just roll away. Then a thought ran across her mind, one that she didn't think she had to worry about for awhile. Maybe Kellie wouldn't want too.

At the pizza parlor, Eric opened the door for Kellie as she waved to her mom.

"See ya in two hours," said Mrs. Jones.

"Yeah mom thanks, see ya."

"I really love the pizza here," said Eric. "I hope you don't think it's gross, but I like anchovies and pineapple on mine."

"Gross? That's what I eat on my pizza too only I also put hot pepper flakes on it. Maggz always says that my stomach is made of iron."

"I'll have to try that." They ordered and Eric took two sodas over to the table.

They began playing straw hockey hitting sugar packets across the table with their straws, when Jade walked in. Her fake dyed blond hair was in a purposely messy French twist. Her pink mini skirt had silver glitter on it, which matched her platform sandals, silver lip gloss and fake nails. She looked like she was going to a club instead of picking up a pizza pie. Kellie actually heard Jade before she saw her. Jade was snapping that sickly sweet smelling wad of gum while gossiping on her cell phone. She was with her right hand girl Sora Hayashi. Kellie was always interested in the meaning behind names. She liked unusual names for the characters she wrote about in her own stories. She looked Sora's up on the Internet and found out it means "sky forest".

To Kellie, the English translation of Sora's name was in sharp contrast to Sora, who was book smart, but didn't seem that deep. She copied Jade's way of dress and mannerisms. Sora looked like she was in fear all the time, like a squirrel, who forgot where they hid the nuts for winter survival. Small Sora looked lost next to tall Jade. Kellie thought to herself, "Maybe, she got lost in her own forest."

Eric saw Kellie's distracted look and followed Kellie's gaze across the room toward the door behind him, "Hey Jade, Sora pull up a seat. I want you to meet a friend of mine."

Jade snapped her pink phone closed with one hand. She and Sora came to the table, but didn't bring chairs with them. Kellie was relieved. Maybe they wouldn't stay.

"Hey, Eric!" said Jade. "Yeah, we've met before, Kellie right?"

Kellie couldn't believe how sweet Jade sounded, but she knew better then to fall for it. In fact, as the words rolled out of Jade's mouth she swore she saw a forked tongue pop out. Kellie knew this meeting would bite her in the ass at a later date.

"So what brings you two here?" Jade's jealousy was flaring up, but she looked cool in front of Eric. She knew he was always nice to the charity cases.

"I just got out of soccer class with the kids and Kellie just got out of swim practice."

"YOU swim?" Jade wanted to make a nasty comment, but she was smart enough to hold back since it wouldn't serve her well.

"Yes, I'm hoping to return to competing." Kellie was hoping she wouldn't ask anymore and would just take her pizza and her little friend and get out of their faces.

Thankfully, Jade was too self absorbed to question anymore.

"Well, I was thinking of going to the movies tonight Eric, so you should really go home soon and rest up. I'll be ready at 7 p.m."

"Uh, well. I..." Eric felt bad. What should he do? How can he make a date in front of another date? I mean Kellie was just a friend...but he wasn't really sure she would stay just a friend. Girls are so complicated he thought to himself.

"I'll give you a call when I get home, OK?" Eric held his breath hoping this was the right answer.

"Sure, no prob. If I don't hear from you by 6:30 p.m., I'll go without you. Hunter said he'd take me."
Eric couldn't stand Hunter Davis. He was a sleazy football player, who was more interested in scoring with a girl and once he was done with her he was on to the next. He couldn't let Jade go with him! She's too good for him.
Jade grabbed a loose curl of hair and twirled it around her fake nail. "Well, see ya around."

Sora, who didn't do anything but grin the whole time said with a staccato Japanese accent, "See you 'round." Sora admired Jade too much to realize that she was being used. Jade knew Kellie didn't like her so she asked Sora to friend Kellie on Buddybook. That way, Jade, who was Sora's Buddybook contact could she what she was up to and she could keep an eye on Eric.

When they both left, Kellie put the straw in her mouth and concentrated hard on her soda. She was trying to avoid the shocked look on Eric's face.

"I can't believe she would go out with that octopus," said Eric.

"Well, I guess you'd better go home and rest up for your movie date. I hear it takes a lot of energy to go to the movies these days." Oops, Kellie couldn't help sounding sarcastic. It slipped out so quickly she was even surprised.

"I know what you're thinkin'." Eric tossed the straw he was twisting on the table.

"Umm, how would you know what I'm thinking? We have yet to have a full conversation. You don't know me well enough." Kellie hoped that would close the subject, too late.

"You think she's manipulating me, but you don't know Jade," said Eric.

"I know the type, she said rolling her eyes. "Look, I don't really know you either. I shouldn't be butting in." Kellie looked out the window hoping to see her mom's car. No such luck. She could go to the bathroom and call her on her cell, but she didn't want to seem like a baby.

"I think you're smart and you're an outsider at school so you don't know the truth about Jade."

"Thanks a lot buddy." said Kellie.

"I don't mean it that way. You have to understand most of us grew up together. We are so close we know each other's birth weight and around here it's expected that Jade is my girlfriend, you know?"

"No, I don't know." Kellie was growing impatient. "When someone shows no respect for you and your time, why should you bother with them?"

"She's the head cheerleader and I'm the star soccer player, so people think we should be together."

"Wow, I wasn't aware that was on the sports permission slip. I can't let her go out with that wacko Hunter. He lives up to his name you know, he hunts girls down and leaves them like road kill."

"Listen, one thing I've learned since I lost my leg is you make your own choices in life."

"Your mom told me about the accident and all." Eric took a bite of his pizza.

"Did she tell you that I blamed everybody at first? I didn't want to say anything because I didn't want to hurt my friend, Tara. Her cousin shouldn't have been driving.

"I know, your mom said the driver dropped a cell phone."

"That's right, but Dean also drank alcohol before picking us up. He caused the accident that made me lose my leg. But in the end, I made the decision to accept the ride. I put myself in danger because I was too worried about embarrassing him and hurting my friend Tara's feelings. I'll never do it again because my life is worth more than that. So you need to decide. Are you with Jade because everyone else wants you to be with her? Is it because you want to rescue her from the bad parts of her life or do you really like being with her?"

"Wow that's deep Miss Kellie."

"Not bad for an outsider, huh?"

"So what are you doing this weekend?" Eric was hoping she would be available for another buddy date."

"Tomorrow I'm going to hang out at the mall with Maggie and Susan. They want to get a jump start on school clothes shopping. Yeah, I know, school just ended. But the two of them don't need much encouragement. I'm hoping to get a prosthetic leg soon so that it will be worthwhile to buy jeans."

"So you'll be able to walk? No more wheelchair?"

"Yup. I'm nervous about it, but I'm more excited than scared so that's a good thing. It's kind of the way I felt about starting swim lessons today. But I shouldn't get my hopes up. The insurance company rejected me already."

"What? That's crazy!"

"I know, but Maggie seems to think that they will change their mind. She keeps sending them her whirlies."

"Her what?"

"Her whirlies, that's her word for good thoughts."

"Have they worked before?"

"Well, they usually work for Math tests."

"Then , I think we need to celebrate for when her whirlies work. How about another slice?" Eric was already half way out of his seat.

Kellie reached for Eric's arm to stop him instead she knocked over his almost empty cup of soda. He grabbed some napkins at the next table and tossed it on the small amount of liquid.

"Sorry about that. Anyway, I don't know if I should eat anymore I've got to watch what I eat now that I'm in training."

"Think of it as payment for your good advice, Dimples."

"What did you call me?"

"Dimples, you have them when you smile. They're cute."

"Oh, cute, yeah I guess so."

"Listen, your mom won't be back for another 30 minutes, so I've got some more questions to ask. I need to keep you well fed as I pick your brain."

"OK, but this next session is going to cost you some extra cheese."

"You've got it."

CHAPTER TWELVE

LEAVING PROBLEMS OUT ON
THE SOCCER FIELD

The next day, Eric dropped the soccer ball on to his knee and then bounced it to the other knee. The soccer ball is part of Eric like his leg or an arm he always has it with him. Soccer makes sense to him. Other things like his father and girls he will never understand. Bam, putter, putter, putter. Bam goes the ball against the garage door.

Eric's father, a suit wearing guy (even on weekends) leans out the window of his study. "Eric the garage is not your personal goal net. Don't you have to mow a lawn or something?"

"Nope" said Eric kicking the ball.

There was a time when Eric would have asked his dad to join him. Eric's dad would choose one of two excuses, "Gotta get this budget done." or "Cash doesn't grow on trees, kid. I gotta work."

By the time he turned 12, Eric stopped asking. Eric bumped the ball off his head. As he looked up he could see his dad straightening his orange cotton tie. The one he always wore on Saturdays.

"Then go to the park or get a job will ya?"

Eric took the ball in his arms and looked up at the window. "I have a paper route and mow lawns, remember?"

"You can do better than that," said Mr. Green. "You're old enough to take responsibility."

That last jab made Eric really mad. That's why Eric always chose to play. He figured there would be plenty of time to work after college. In fact, it seems adults never stop working so why bother rushing into it?

Eric's mom was always working too. The two incomes made them more than comfortable. The Greens owned a beautiful home designed by his dad in the Painted Aprons section of Port Jervis. Port was made up of mostly old Victorians in need of fixing, trailer homes and apartments with lazy landlords. Painted Aprons had modern housing; you know the kind with solar panels and log cabin design. Still, Abe Lincoln never stayed in this type of log cabin. The Greens had the best of everything and they thought they were being good parents by giving Eric, his older brother, Tommy, and his little brother, Danny, all the material things in life.

Eric picked up the ball and said "I'll be at Riverside Creamery, dad."

"All right, no more than two hours. Your mom wants you home before dinner."

Eric laughed to himself. Why would he have to be home for dinner? They never ate at the same time anyway. The last time they ate together was last Christmas. Usually mom had a crock pot of stew boiling and everyone took a bowl of it on their own. Or they ate soup and sandwiches with everyone scattered throughout the house.

Eric volleyed the soccer ball from right to left foot all the way down East Main Street. When he got to Pike Street he made a left and held the ball while walking down the steep hill.

He saw Jade coming out of Port Java with her friends holding a cookie. He ducked on the side of a building until they passed him.

They've been going out for a year, a very long year. Jade, a football cheerleader, started going to soccer games

65

when she broke up with her linebacker boyfriend. Jade wasn't Eric's type really, but she seemed to always be around. They started talking after his soccer games and meeting at Homer's Coffee Shop for a bite to eat. Before Eric knew it, Jade told everyone he was her boyfriend. At first, Eric didn't mind. Jade was popular, flashy and pretty. Any high school boy would say he was crazy to refuse her. But soon, Eric realized Jade had lots of problems at home. He was caught in the middle and unprepared to deal with her father's abuse. Eric decided that he would continue to see Jade to keep her away from her father - at least on the weekends. Eric always took Jade to late movies so that by the time she got home, her dad was passed out on the couch.

He wanted to tell Jade's police chief uncle, his parents or a teacher about the abuse, but Jade begged him not to.

Jade was always sweet to him, but Eric heard she had a mean streak. One of his teammates said Jealousy should have been her name not Jade. But Eric just thought he was jealous. Still, he remembers getting reamed by Jade the day he sat next to Kellie at a basketball game and showed her how to spin the ball on her finger.

Yup, Eric definitely felt like a fish caught in a net. If he got away, what good would it do him? He would still have a painful rusty hook in his mouth since he would be abandoning Jade just like everyone else did in her life.

CHAPTER THIRTEEN

SWEET SORA

Sora Hayashi is a member of the Jaded gang. Well sort of. It's a trial thing and she knows it. Her whole life has been a trial since she moved to the U.S. from Japan two years ago. As she looks through her closet at the red kimono with gold threads intertwined in hues of blue and green she thinks about Yuko, her closest friend in Tokyo. They did everything together from the time they met at age seven in a public swimming pool.

Yuko was taller than Sora and slender with long silky hair down to her waist. As they reached 13, the boys started noticing Yuko. They didn't notice Sora as much, but at least she got some attention since she was Yuko's friend. Yuko was unaware of her beauty and never considered Sora second best. To Yuko, Sora was smart. She could solve math problems faster than anyone in the class. Her short course hair would fall in her face and cover her glasses every time she tipped her head down to write. But behind the glasses and buck teeth that glittered from her wearing braces was a person with wisdom. Even at such a young age, Yuko looked up to Sora. She would trade her looks in a minute for an ounce of Sora's intelligence. They weren't sisters by blood, but sometimes blood isn't needed to feel related.

Sora twirled a bubble gum pink and white fan lying on her dresser. She tossed it in the air and caught it with one hand and in one full flick of her wrist it opened. Sitting down on her bed she studied the cherry blossom pattern and traced the pleats with her fingers.

It was the last gift Yuko gave to Sora before she went to America. Yuko said it would remind her of home. At the airport, Sora took the fan and handed Yuko a letter. In it she told her how much she wanted to run away. How she wished her father never got a better job and how guilty she felt for even saying that. The Huyengs were poor in Japan. Her father was offered a chance to triple his salary in the United States. Her mother wouldn't have to work as a cleaning lady anymore. It was a no brainer for her father. But it was the worst possible move for Sora.

When the Huyengs came to Port Jervis, Sora knew she wouldn't fit in. Sure, she knew English. All Japanese students learn to read and write English. She scored high on all of the comprehension tests too. She soon learned that book smarts meant nothing against street smarts. The English the Japanese taught her wasn't what she needed to blend in with the American kids.

The first day of school, Sora clutched her freshman handbook in her hand. A kid with baggy jeans sucking on his pencil was leaning against her locker. He said he was new to the school and asked her what's the down low on the smoke room? Sora only understood the down low part so she squatted down on the ground right in the hallway.

"What is your problem?" he said. "I said so what's the "down low" on the smoke room?

The kids called it the smoke room. It was an old bathroom on the top floor that was rarely used. The kids would open the windows, stand on the toilets inside the stall, crouch down and smoke. The hall monitors only checked underneath the stall doors for feet whenever they smelled smoke and there was always a look-out to warn the kids and distract the monitors.

Sora didn't know anything about the smoke room. And she still didn't understand the whole question, so she continued to squat.

"What's wrong which ya? You hafta use the bathroom or somethin?" shouted Baggy Boy. Everyone stopped and all eyes looked at her.

"Thanks for nothin' Potty Princess. I'll figure it out on my own."

Laughter bounced off the walls like a pinball ricocheting off the leavers and bells in a pinball machine. That's how she got her nickname. No one called her Sora; it was just "Potty Princess" after that. She didn't even know what a potty was because she kept spelling it "poddy" and couldn't find it in her Japanese to English dictionary. She finally figured it out after two days of random people laughing while grabbing her hand and dragging her to the bathroom.

Math class was the only time Sora felt confident since numbers are universal all over the world. That's where she met her new best friend, Jade Santiago, also a sophomore, who sat next to her in math. She was so pretty. Her nails were painted in purple with silver glitter on them. Sora allowed Jade to copy off of her math tests and Jade got everyone to stop calling her "Potty Princess". Jade had power and protected her like Yuko. People stopped when Jade walked in a room. She was just like Yuko, at least that's what Sora thought.

CHAPTER FOURTEEN

WHAT'S HIS MOTIVE?

Kellie waved goodbye to Eric as her mom pressed the button for her chair lift so that she could get into the car.

"Did you have a nice time?"

"Yes, but I'm stuffed. I really gorged on the pizza." Her mother got into the driver side of the car, fastened her seat belt and started the car.

"I have to pick Maggie up in two hours. I hope her first day at her summer job went well."

"At least she won't spend her paycheck at the Book Nook. Thank God she didn't get that clothing store job," said Kellie as she adjusted the top of her seat belt.

"So Eric seems like a nice kid, does he know Maggie well too?" Mrs. Jones was fishing to find out whether or not this Eric kid really wanted to date Maggie. She worried that Kellie might get hurt if he was just trying to butter her up to get to Maggie.

"Not really. He knows Susan a little better since he likes to eat ice cream. Susan says he's one of her best customers. He can scarf down two of those large thick shakes in one sitting and yet he's a toothpick. If I ate like that I'd be huge."

"Well, since you are swimming again you won't have to worry as much about your weight. You'll have to eat more, not less."

"Does Maggie like Eric?" Mrs. Jones knew she had to be careful here, but there must be some reason a teen athlete is interested in a disabled girl.

"She thinks he's a nice person and a good soccer player, but that's all she ever said about him. Why mom, what's the deal with the 20 questions?"

Mrs. Jones began to sweat. Should she tell Kellie why she was suspicious and risk hurting her in order to protect her? Or should she just watch the relationship carefully.

"I don't know, Kellie, you know how guys are."

"No, how are they?" Kellie was starting to grow a little angry.

"Kellie, I'm just concerned. This Eric kid may have the best intentions, but a teen athlete like him always dates the perfect girl."

"And?" Kellie knew what her mother was getting at, but she wanted her to say it.

Mrs. Jones just blurted it out as quickly as she could "And you don't have a leg so what if he is only dating you to get to Maggie?"

"Why can't you just give me a little credit? You know mom, even before I lost my leg I always knew you thought Maggie was the prettier one and now you have proved it. You always played favorites and the only attention I EVER got was BECAUSE I lost my leg. You think that makes me HAPPY?"

"Kellie that's not true. You are just as pretty as Maggie. It's just that a teenage boy wants perfection, especially, an athlete." Mrs. Jones could see she wasn't making any progress. Kellie's face was all red, tears were flowing and Mrs. Jones couldn't take it back.

"Kellie I love you and I want what is best for you. I just want you to think about it."

"You know mom Eric is NOT my boyfriend. He is Jade's boyfriend, which to be honest I think is a bad

71

choice, but I won't go there with you. Still, you can't even be proud that I finally made a friend other than Maggie and Susan. Susan is really Maggz friend anyway. I have no one here and you don't care."

"Wait a second, I do care. I was happy that you went to lunch with this boy. I just don't want to see you hurt."

"Well, you did a good job of doing that yourself!" As their car pulled into the driveway, Kellie wished more than ever that she had her prosthetic limb. She wanted to run out of the car and into the house slamming the door behind her. She wanted to leap up the stairs and go in her room and hide. She wanted to run away, but she couldn't. Instead she waited for her mother to get out of the car, get the chair lift down so that Kellie could get out of the car. Her mom followed as they went up the ramp and Kellie rolled into the door. She almost rolled over her father's toes as he came to greet them at the door.

"What's the trouble little bubble?" said Harold. Kellie didn't answer. So Harold turned to his wife "what happened?"

Kellie grabbed her crutches and was navigating the staircase as fast as possible. This wasn't easy, but she was determined.

Mrs. Jones looked at her husband "I'm always to blame. She always misunderstands what I say. I guess that Mom of the Year award won't come to me this year."

Harold, like many fathers, just wasn't great with handling tears. He would often tell the girls they were too sensitive. It was mainly because it broke his heart to see them upset.

Mrs. Jones explained the whole incident between sobs.

"Shirley, come on. Of course she's crushed. She's just a kid. I know you care, but you have to let her find out if this kid has ulterior motives on her own."

"I just wanted to plant the idea. You know boys can't be trusted."

"Hey, thanks!" Harold knew she didn't mean him. But he couldn't resist.

"You know what I mean. But as usual, she doesn't so I think I should to go up there and talk to her." Mrs. Jones climbed the stairs and knocked on Kellie's door.

"Don't come in." Kellie sobbed.

"I come in peace," laughed Mrs. Jones. Silence.

Mrs. Jones opened the door a crack. "Come on Kellie I just want to talk."

"I guess I can't stop you since I'm not perfect to begin with," Kellie fumed. "The door is unlocked anyway and by the time I got up you would have been able to come in anyway."

Mrs. Jones took the stuffed animals on Kellie's bed and put them on her rocking chair. She sat down on the side of the bed. "You're right. You aren't perfect and neither am I. I shouldn't have been so insensitive. I'm glad you found a friend and I shouldn't jump to conclusions. I was just trying to protect you. It's my job, I'm your mom and I'm sorry."

"Mom, what if you are right? I'm not perfect. Look at me."

"So, if I'm right then, who cares? You have one physical imperfection Kellie. Some people have so many they can't count them. Others are just rotten people to begin with. What's important is you are a wonderful, smart and beautiful girl. Those are your good qualities and

73

they far outweigh the loss of your leg. If Eric doesn't see it or other people don't see it, that's their problem."

"I guess so, you got me thinkin' though," sighed Kellie.

"That's all I wanted to do. I just want you to be aware, that's all. But most importantly, have a good time and I happen to think that Susan is a good friend to both of you."

"I guess. Her mom offered to take us to the mall on Sunday. Susan says Mr. Reynolds asked her mom to breakfast next Saturday since it's his only time off from the creamery."

"Oh that's wonderful. Mrs. Fydrych is such a great lady. She needs a little happiness in her life. And Mr. Reynolds is a kind man."

"Yeah, but Mrs. Fydrych told him she would let him know. She really wanted to ask Susan first if it bothered her. Susan told her mom to go for it so Mrs. Fydrych accepted and now wants to browse the stores to see if she can get a new outfit."

"So are you girls going to help her?" said Mrs. Jones.

"I guess. She doesn't speak English that well. So I think that's why she was afraid to go on the date."

"See, Kellie she has her imperfections too." They both laughed.

CHAPTER FIFTEEN

THESE BOOTS ARE MADE FOR WALKIN'

Mrs. Fydrych parked the car in the mall parking lot. She got Kellie's collapsed wheelchair out of the car and Maggie opened it up and brought around the car to Kellie. They went straight into the mall's entrance and wandered for awhile through stark white corridor and looked through the store windows.

Then Kellie saw them her dream boots. They were black leather with a small, but slender heel. They hit below the knee with three silver buckles on either side of the boot. They looked similar to the ones worn at the beginning of the movie "The Devil Wears Prada," just not as long and as her mom would say "vampy".

Maggie came up behind her. "Wow, those are smokin'. Let's go in and see how much they are." Susan said something to her mom in Polish and took her mom by the arm as the girls and Mrs. Fydrych went in to explore. Maggie flipped over the boot to see the price. "A hundred and twenty bucks! Man, do they come with the cow too?"

Mrs. Fydrych looked at Susan. Susan didn't even bother translating anything besides the price to her mom. Mrs. Fydrych's eyes widened. Sora came out of the back room balancing four stacked boxes that hid her face. She put them down on the floor and began to put them on the shelf when she saw Kellie. She walked up to the group as they were talking among each other.

"Forget it. That's way too much out of the back to school clothing allowance mom and dad gave us. Too bad though. I was looking forward to a pair of boots when I get the prosthesis."

"Hell-o Kel-ly, 'member me? We met at pizza place." Sora chose her words carefully.

"Hi Sora of course I remember. Since you are a year ahead of us, you've probably never met my twin sister, Maggie, and our friend Susan. And this is Susan's mom, Mrs. Fydrych."

"Nice to meet you," said Sora then her eyes searched the store. Her boss didn't like it when his employees talked too long with the customers. Sora rarely got into trouble since her English was still shaky so she hated to talk to customers.

"Do you work here?" said Maggie as she noticed Sora's name tag. Maggie had a tinge of envy in her voice. What she wouldn't give to be around so many shoes.

"Yes, I work here six month now," said Sora. "Can I help you?"

"We were just admiring these boots. I haven't worn boots since my accident. But now I'm hoping the insurance will approve my prosthesis. So I maybe I will be able to wear them after all."

"Prosthesis?" Sora lifted her eyebrow. This was not a word she knew and she wouldn't even begin to know where to find it in the Japanese to English dictionary she had in her back pocket at all times.

"Yeah, I'm getting a fake leg so that I can walk like everyone else."

"Wow!" said Sora with wide eyes. "So what your size?"

"Thanks, but they're way too much money," said Kellie as she stared at the shiny buckles.

"We have sale soon. I can put it away," said Sora already walking towards the boxes underneath the sample boot.

"Try one boot on Kellie and see how it feels. Then she can put them aside and we can talk to mom about them," said Maggie.

Kellie slipped on a 7 1/2 and with help from Maggie she stood on the one leg. "Wow, it feels great. But it's too much." She sat back in her chair as Sora pulled off the boot and put it back in the box.

"Thanks Sora. I guess we'll see you around." Kellie said then they began to leave the store. Maggie held the door for Kellie. She saw her linger behind a little looking at the boots. Then she rolled out the door. Sora took them with her in the back and put Kellie's name on them hoping that she would be back.

After a long day in and out of the stores, Mrs. Fydrych said, "Girls, ice cream. I treat."

"No, Mrs. Fydrych. We can buy our own," Maggie and Kellie protested. They knew about her money troubles.

"No, no I buy. Let me." Mrs. Fydrych sighed and said something in Polish to Susan.

"Guys really, let her buy it. My mom will feel insulted if you don't accept it."

"OK, just a small cone. I'm training you know."

"Yeah me too, I'm training to get into that pink plaid skirt at The Limited," laughed Maggie. They sat at the table in the food court and laughed, ate and talked.

"So when is your first swim meet?" Susan said in between licks of her vanilla ice cream cone that was melting fast.

"This Tuesday and I'm so nervous."

"Any news about the prosthetic leg?" said Susan.

"Nope, not yet, which is another thing that is driving me crazy my mom sent in the appeal letter weeks ago."

"So, if you get approved soon, by the time you go back to school, you'll be walking?" Susan wiped her hands with a napkin.

"Yup, she'll strut behind Jade and say "Boo"! Maggie flipped back her head in a roar of laughter. "I can't wait to see her face. You know Sue, Kellie already met with Eric for pizza and who do you think saw them?"

"No!" Susan's blue eyes tripled in size. Mrs. Fydrych sat there smiling. She could only keep up with some of what they were saying. Susan always felt bad about that because her mom was super smart, but in a different language it was like starting from scratch. Susan translated a little to her mom.

"Eric and I are just friends. Don't get any ideas," said Kellie.

"Oh we don't have to." Susan smiled. "I'm sure Jade already has them and she deserves every last one of them."

CHAPTER SIXTEEN

GOOD NEWS COMES TO THOSE WHO WAIT

"Cookies!" Maggie ran and picked one off the plate.

"Wait just a minute Maggie Mae. These cookies are for after dinner. We need to celebrate."

"Celebrate what?" moaned Kellie.

"I got the letter from the insurance in the mail today." Shirley smiled. "Kellie, you were approved!"
Maggie dropped her cookie on the floor and screamed, jumping up and down. You would have thought the leg was for her.

"Are they covering the whole thing?" said Kellie in disbelief knowing that her parents couldn't afford it.

"Of course, they're covering the whole thing. What do you think, Ding Dong that they would only give you HALF A LEG?" teased Maggie.

"Well, in a way they are since it's below my knee!" laughed Kellie.

Harold walked into the kitchen at that moment. "What's all the shouting here. You girls have got to get along better than this."

"Harold, Kellie's insurance approval came through. She can get her prosthesis now." Shirley said showing him the letter.

"That's the best news I heard all day," said Harold. "And we better move quickly because there are rumors of layoffs at the company. I'm not one of them - yet."

"Uh oh." said Kellie.

"Never mind, this is terrific news, little doll. It's a whole new beginning for you." Harold reached for a cookie and Shirley gave him the same sideways scowl she used on the girls when they misbehaved. Harold put it down immediately.

"You know what this means, Maggz?" Kellie snatched the letter from her mother.

"What?"

"I'll be stealing both your shoes instead of one." They all laughed as Kellie stared some more at the letter in disbelief.

How much good luck could one person have Kellie thought first a pizza date (or a buddy get together) with Eric, a new swim coach and now a new leg.

After dinner, Kellie went to her room, got ready for bed and boosted herself from her chair into her bed. She turned to the side to look at her wheelchair. Empty now, with its red seat cushion it almost looked sad. Wow, how different it will be when I can just walk into my room, she thought. She called Tara and then Susan to tell them the news. Then when she called Eric on his cell and Jade answered.

Jade was in a happy mood. She finally knew what she would do. Jade and Sora met for a soda at Homer's Coffee Shop on Sunday. That's when Sora told Jade about Kellie's new leg. Sora was so happy for Kellie. She just wanted to share the news with her best friend. But Jade saw it as an opportunity to get back at the bitch that stole her boyfriend. Or at least is in the process of stealing him. That night, when they went out to the movies; Eric was in another world. He asked Jade if she wanted popcorn, but accidentally called her Kellie!

Jade ignored it, but knew she would have to publicly embarrass Kellie and make her look like a Dingleberry in front of Eric, but how? That night, she called Hunter and they went over to the creamery. She watched as Hunter inhaled the triple scoop sundae she bought him. What a pig she thought, but she had to be nice to Hunter so they could carry out their plan. Actually, Jade planned while Hunter ate and struggled to remember what he had to do to this Kellie girl on the first day of school. Jade took Hunter's hand, but was interrupted by this Little Mermaid look-a-like waitress, who kept popping up out of no where to ask if everything was OK.

"Yes, the food is fine; the water is fine now here's your tip and skate that way will ya?" Jade gave her a fake grin.

"Sorry, just doin' my job," said Mary-Chris. She didn't know Jade well, but she knew now not to tick her off. Still, she heard Kellie's name mentioned so she stayed close pretending to clean the tables. It was then that Mary-Chris heard about Jade's plan. Mary-Chris didn't know Kellie well either. She even heard Kellie making fun of her praying with Susan. Still, Kellie seemed like a decent person and her sister, Maggie might make a good friend. Should she warn Kellie, or stay out of it?

CHAPTER SEVENTEEN

TWO LEFT FEET!

The Jones Family walked into the prosthetics office in Goshen. Mr. and Mrs. Jones and Maggie took the day off from work for this. All of them didn't have to be there, but they wanted to understand what was needed to be done and it was a big moment for the family. Kind of like Kellie was getting an award. Mrs. Jones walked up to the receptionist's window. "We have an appointment with Ms. Thompson at 11 a.m.?" The receptionist peered over her half glasses with her small brown eyes. "Sure, why don't you take a seat? She will be with you in a moment."

As Kellie waited she thought about Jade's voice at the other end of Eric's cell phone. "Don't jump to conclusions," she said to herself, but it made her angry. A few minutes passed then a woman came into the waiting room. "Kellie Jones? Hi, I'm Kim Thompson, but just call me Kim. Why don't you all follow me and we will measure Kellie for her prosthesis." They went into a large room with a bunch of couches in it. In the corner was a metal apparatus with railings on it so that people could try out their new legs.

"So your staples were taken out a long time ago and your stump is not swollen. That's good. Are you ready for your temporary prosthesis?" asked Kim as she got out the measuring tape.

"She's not getting the permanent one?" Mrs. Jones looked more disappointed then Kellie.

"Sure she will. But first we make a temporary prosthesis. Your permanent one will take about four trial fittings to make it perfect and that will take a few weeks. The temporary one takes about a week to make. Kellie, could you stand up so I can measure you?"

Kim took the measuring tape and placed it at the center of Kellie's good leg. She stretched it from the knee to the edge of her foot. Then she did the same with her missing leg and wrote the measurements down. "You have good balance so that should help you learn to walk with the new leg."

"I'll tell Coach Eileen you said that." Kellie grinned.

"Who's Coach Eileen?" Kim asked.

"She's my swim coach. I'm training to compete for the Paralympics. Is this new leg waterproof and how much does it weigh? I don't want to walk around like I'm dragging a boulder."

"No it's not waterproof and I wouldn't take it in the shower either. But you can order a waterproof covering for the Pylon part of your leg or you can get a waterproof prosthetic. I'm not sure if your insurance would cover it though because it's expensive and not a necessity. I would just bring your crutches to the pool and swim without it for now. Today, prosthetic legs are light. They will only be about one sixth of your body weight," said Kim as she brought out a model to show Kellie how to clean the prosthesis socket. "This is the socket and it should be cleaned with a towel after using the leg. You will have a suction socket so the limb will attach onto your stump by suction. Clean the socket each night with a wet towel and make sure your stump is clean and free of sores or blisters. If redness persists for more than 20 minutes you have to call your doctor. This is serious because you don't want an infection."

"How long will it take for me to get used to walking with two legs?" Kellie wanted to run down the street this second. She wanted to be free from taking help from everyone.

"You should be up and around in a week, but it's different for everyone. It may take a month before you feel confident," said Kim.

"Can she wear heels?" said Maggie. Of course fashion was always Maggie's biggest concern. But she really felt bad for Kellie. She wanted her to fit in at school even if it meant that she would be stealing both of Maggie's shoes.

"Sure, there is an adjustable heel on the foot of the leg. You can wear any type of well made shoe. How old are you, Kellie?"

"I will turn 15 next week, but this is the best birthday gift ever."

"That's wonderful," said Kim. "But according to your age, you aren't done growing yet."

"Oh, she's short alright and that's the way she'll stay." Maggie laughed.

"Maybe, but she may still grow a few inches and over time you will gain and lose weight so you will need to go for a check up every six months. I've got all the information I need. Do you have any other questions?"

"Yeah, when can I get my leg?"

"That's the most important thing and I didn't answer it. Sorry about that. We will call you as soon as it comes in. I expect it to be next Monday."

"Woo Hoo! I wish I could jump up and click my heels," laughed Kellie.

"Oh you will, don't worry you will." said Kim.

CHAPTER EIGHTEEN

READY, SET, SWIM

"You can do it, Miss Risk. Now remember when you're out there, focus on reaching diving in and reaching for the other end of the pool. That will give you the best start. Tuck your head down before diving in and remember don't look at the others when you turn your head to take a breath. Now, touch the pool railing as you hop up with your crutches to the edge of the pool and leave your worries at the railing." Coach Eileen said with confidence. This was only one of the Paralympics qualifying swim meets, but Kellie was a determined kid and a tough competitor.

"I don't know. What if...?" Kellie could feel the nerves eating at her. She began to tremble and her eyes were tearing.

"How could you fail? You showed up right?" Eileen grabbed onto her shoulder and bent down to look in her eyes.

"Right!" cried Kellie.

"That's half the battle. Now, all you have to do is your best and then you've won." Eileen could hear herself saying the famous words from director, Woody Allen, she just wasn't sure Kellie was listening to them.

A man on a microphone blew his whistle and announced that the contestants for the freestyle should take their places at poolside. This was the last race of the day. Poor Kellie had to wait all this time.

"Oh God, that's me!" Kellie looked up into the stands and saw her whole family, Susan and her mom. They all started waving at her. Eric was in the stands too, but Kellie didn't know that. It was a good thing too since that would have really made her jittery. Today is August 5th, the twin's fifteenth birthday. Kellie silently hoped that it would bring her luck.

"Shake out your hands and arms. You'll be fine. Let me help you to the pool and I will take your crutches when you are ready." Eileen gave Kellie a tissue and a pat on the back. They made it to pool side and Kellie was lucky to get a spot near the railing. She grabbed onto it and tried to leave all her anxiety there.

She let go as the announcer said, on your mark, get set" and then blew the whistle.

Kellie tucked her head and reached out just as Eileen told her plunging, into the tepid water. Kellie took the lead.

She glided for the required 15 meters and then began to do the front crawl, staying almost flat with a flutter kick. Her arms alternated bending at the elbow and lifting up and back. As she lifted her head to the side she could hear the screaming and cheering. She got to the wall, tucked and rolled, pushing her one foot forward to push against the wall while on her back. Then she rolled over and continued the front crawl for the last leg of the race. She didn't know it but she was neck and neck with the girl to the left of her.

Coach Eileen's legs were so stiff with excitement her knees locked. She wanted Kellie to win so badly because she knew this would stoke her confidence.

Kellie made the mistake of looking at the other girl when she turned her head and the breath she took wasn't enough. She started to panic under the water knowing she would need to take an extra puff of air, this could put her behind.

86

Eileen saw Kellie lose her speed momentarily.

Maggie saw her falter too. "Damn, come on," she muttered under her breath.

Then in a burst of strength, Kellie's leg came through. She gave two extra strong flutter kicks put her hand out and touched the wall just a two seconds before the girl to her left.

The first thing she saw was Coach Eileen jumping up and down and running (which she wasn't supposed to do) on the pool deck. She reached for Kellie to help her out of the water, hugged her. Then Eileen told her to raise her right hand to the crowd in victory while the announcer said Kellie's name as the winner.

"I won?" Kellie's green saucer size eyes tripled in size with disbelief. "Oh my God, I won."

"You sure did Miss Risk. Good girl!"

Kellie sat down on the side as her family, Susan and her mother made their way down to the pool. Kellie draped a towel around her shoulders and began to chatter a bit. She took a swig from her water bottle.

"Kell you were awesome, girl. I wasn't sure ya had it in ya." Susan grinned. "But I guess a little bit of Brooklyn rubbed off on ya. I should attend these meets every time."

Kellie reached out to hug Susan. "You'd better. I needed to see you in the stands."

"Did you see me?" Kellie's mom wanted to be sure Kellie knew she was proud.

"Ma, not only could I see you, but I could hear you even when I was under water." They all laughed. Mrs. Jones was known for her loud shouts.

"You did great little doll." Kellie's dad, a quiet guy, wasn't big into hugging or making grand statements. But what he said that day was equivalent to a million hugs. Meanwhile, Maggie continued to squeeze the life out of Kellie.

"Hey, what's in that huge bag?" Kellie said as she sat on the bench.

"It's for you from Susan, Mary-Chris, Sora and me." Kellie looked up at her parents, who didn't seem to know what Maggie was talking about.

"Come on open it," Susan said as Kellie sat back down in the chair. By now everyone left the bleachers and the crowd was out in the hall. Kellie removed the hot pink bow and stuck it on top of her wet swim cap. She tore the blue paper carefully.

"Stop being so neat," Mrs. Jones said. She was interested too. She had her own gift for her, an ID bracelet that was engraved with "Miss Risk" on it. Inside it said "You can do it". She was going to give it to her at dinner, but she had no idea what the girls had for Kellie.

Kellie popped the top of the white box open and there they were. Those beautiful black leather boots with the silver buckles that she admired in the store. "Oh my God, you guys, this is too much!"

"Sora stashed them in the back after we left and called me when they went on sale. She said if they don't fit properly with your new leg, you can bring them back." Maggie was excited and also happy she got a heads up on a good sale to her it was like winning a gold medal.

"We all chipped in for them because we knew how much you loved them. Sora gave us her discount on top of the sale and Mary-Chris gave me her tip money when she heard Maggie and me talking about the boots at the creamery." Susan said with a mile long grin on her face looked just as happy as Kellie.

"Maggie, Susan you are so thoughtful," said Kellie's mom. "Maggie, I think this job has taught you the value of a dollar." Maggie groaned a little. Her mother wasn't going to ever give her complete credit.

What Maggie didn't understand was her mom saw it as a sign that her twins were growing up. Although she wasn't always sure, today she realized her girls were on the right track.

"Look inside the boots, Kell." said Maggie.
Kellie stuck her hand down one of the boots and pulled out a sealed letter from Mary-Chris and a $10 gift certificate for the Port Jervis Pizza parlor.

"That's from Eric, he said he wants to take you out for a victory pizza," said Susan as she twisted a lock of her straight light brown hair. "He drove us to the mall so that we could pick up the boots. He was on his way to the movies, but he was happy to be in on the surprise."

"Hmm...did he go to the movies with Jade again?" Kellie couldn't help but ask.

"I thought you didn't care." said Susan.

"Just curious."

"Nope, it was his dumb brother, Tommy." Susan rolled her eyes and said to the twin's parents. "He's a senior."

"Yeah, Tommy kept asking Susan out and when she refused, he asked me out. The guy is a walking hormone," Maggie was secretly flattered, but she wouldn't date anyone that asked her friend too. That was just gross.

"Thanks guys. I'm so happy. We have to get home so I can try them on with the temporary leg in my room."

Coach Eileen hugged Kellie, gave her a bouquet of flowers and then left. Mr. and Mrs. Jones went to pull the car around and walked Susan and Mrs. Fydrych to the parking lot. Maggie held the box of shoes and Kellie's gym bag and escorted Kellie to the locker room.

After Kellie finished getting dressed in dry clothes and fixed her hair. They walked down the hall together with Kellie swinging through her crutches. She and Maggz were deep into conversation. Maggie was trying to guess what Kellie gave her for her birthday when a deep voice interrupted them.

"Hey Dimples!" Kellie looked up and saw Eric leaning against the wall, his hands in his pockets with one skinny leg bent up against the wall. He looked taller since they last saw each other. The guy never seemed to stop growing. At 16, he was already a lanky 6'1", which was a foot taller than Kellie.

"Hey, thanks so much for the pizza and driving Maggz and Susan. That was so nice."

"It was no big thing. We were already going that way. As for the pizza, there is no excuse now; you have to go out with me...uh again." Eric's cheeks began to redden and his eyes seemed to get even bluer. He realized Maggie was standing right there and he didn't want to seem too eager.

"Sure, I can go for a pizza with my buddy." Kellie was testing the waters. "Should I make an appointment with Jade?"

"Uh, I don't understand, why would you call Jade to go out with me?"

"I called your cell to tell you I got approved for a prosthetic leg and Jade answered."

"That's where my cell phone went." Eric looked down and kicked some imaginary dirt. "Jade broke up with me the other day and I must have left it the cell phone at her house. I don't know. I guess her dad's been drinking

90

again. She got scared and tried to call me, but I wasn't home so she called Hunter instead. I feel bad that I wasn't there for her. Her dad really takes her mom's death out on her and he gets really nasty when he hits the booze. "Jade said she didn't trust that I would be there for her anymore and decided it was better to start her junior year with Hunter, the football star. She traded up I guess."

"Not necessarily," muttered Maggie.

"Look, I understand why you feel bad for her, but you can't be everywhere." Kellie heard her father beep the horn as they walked towards the lobby.

"Kell, I'm really sorry for everything and I'm so happy about your prosthesis and winning the meet. I hope we can still be – buddies."

"School starts in few weeks and I'm going to be busy training for the next meet and learning to walk on the new leg. So I guess I'll see you back at school."

"Uh, I guess so." said Eric a little defeated as he walked the girls to their car and waved at Mrs. Jones. She nodded back at him. The girls got into the car and they took off. Kellie looked out the rear window as Eric got smaller and smaller.

Maggie watched her sister and sighed as she thought to herself, "When is he going to realize how great Kellie is. Man, boys ARE stupid."

CHAPTER NINETEEN

AND WE ALL FALL DOWN

KURPLUNK! Kellie fell in a mound on the floor smacking her butt on the mat below.

"Are you OK?" said Jon the physical therapist helping Kellie adjust to walking with her new leg.

"Yup, I just have a bump on my rump now." Kellie said rubbing her backside. "Let's do it again." Kellie reached for his hands looked up at him and took a deep breath. Her cheeks were red since he Jon was kind of cute.

"Stop it" she said to herself. "Just concentrate and don't be a giant hormone, will ya?".

Jon took her hands and stood in front of her. Coach Eileen came with her mom to be part of the cheering squad.

"One step at a time, Miss Risk. That's all you need to take."

"I'll settle for one step. Whoa!"

"Uh oh, I gotch ya." said Jon. "Oops".

Kellie fell in a heap again. "Maybe something is wrong with the fit. It feels like it's going to fall off."

Kim Thompson, who originally fit the leg, came over to look at the way the leg was fitting to the stump.

"It's fine Kellie. It won't fall off. You just have to trust yourself that's all."

"Maybe we should take a break for today," said Eileen.

"No! I can't spend my life in a wheelchair." Kellie began to tear up.

"You don't have to do it all today." said Kellie's mom. "You were only supposed to stand up. You did that. We'll try again tomorrow."

"Your mom is right Kellie," said Kim. "You've done really well for your first day. It's a tough adjustment. I'm sorry if I made it sound easy. It isn't."

Kellie looked sadly at her wheel chair as Jon helped her toward it. He lowered her in the familiar pink and black striped seat. Again, Kellie felt trapped, dependent upon others. She put her hand on her cheek and leaned her arm on the armrest with despair. Coach Eileen squatted down in front of her grasping the hand rests on the wheelchair.

"Are you and your mom going home after this?"
"I guess."

Eileen looked at Mrs. Jones. "Do you have an extra hour? I want to introduce you to my husband, Sal, he teaches at The Steppin' Up Dance Studio in Milford, Pa."

"Sure, I have the day off so we weren't doing anything after this," said Mrs. Jones. "How about it Kell?"

"OK." Kellie really wanted to go home and pull the covers over her head. She was tired, but more depressed than sleepy.

Kellie and her mother followed Eileen's car to Milford until they parked in front of a stone front building on the corner of Catharine Street. Milford is picturesque with lots of pristine white Colonial mansions converted into businesses. There is one traffic light in the whole town. Most of the businesses had to do with the arts or selling a craft. They even restored an old theater and showed black and white movies at 1950s prices. It would have been a bargain for kids on dates except no one

Kellie's age wanted to watch movies without sound and color.

"Here let me help." Eileen wheeled Kellie up the front ramp and through the front door. Disco music from the 70s was playing and a man and a woman were twirling to the music.

Eileen yelled "Sal are you busy? I have a guest."

The music stopped and a male voice in the next room said "take a break and get some water."

"Eileen is that you honey? Come on in."

Eileen rolled Kellie through the opened wood doors. Her mother followed behind.

"Kellie, Mrs. Jones, I would like you to meet my husband, Sal. He owns this dance studio."

Kellie's mouth fell open as Sal, sitting in his wheelchair, rolled over to meet her.

"Sal was the U.S. Hustle champion. Sal, this is the girl I've been telling you about. Kellie is training for the Paralympics."

"Pleasure to meet you, Kellie, my wife says you are a real go getter and a terrific athlete."

"Thanks, Mr. Foley, but…"

"Oh my last name is Amaranti. Eileen kept her maiden name. It's OK because I fell in love with her Irish eyes anyway," he said putting his arm around Eileen's waist and giving her a squeeze. "Just call me Sal."

Kellie was silent after that. She didn't know how to ask the question, but she was dying to know how Sal could win a dance competition trapped in a wheelchair?

In addition to dancing it seems like Sal was also into reading minds.

"I bet your wondering how I could be a dance champ stuck in this chair?"

94

"Well, yes, I think Kellie is afraid to ask you," Said Mrs. Jones.

"When I was competing I wasn't paralyzed. In fact, would you believe I was once 6' 2"?" He laughed since it was pretty evident that he was a short guy to begin with. "I know I don't look an inch over 5'7" but you can't blame a guy for tryin'.

Sal's grin was contagious and it lifted his long nose when he smiled. His bushy eyebrows framed his kind deep brown eyes. Mrs. Jones decided he was probably much better looking than John Travolta in his younger days.

"After I was diagnosed with muscular dystrophy, I lost feeling in my legs and started to use a cane, then as the disease got worse, I got around by using a set of wheels. But I was really lucky."

"Why?" said Kellie.

"If I hadn't lost the use of my legs I would have never have met Eileen."

"I don't dance and I never have," laughed Eileen. "I met Sal when his doctor recommended taking swimming lessons to strengthen his arms. I taught him how to do the back stroke."

"And she gave me my drive back. I realized dancing wasn't only in the legs. It's in the heart. I opened this dance school and taught people through drawings at first. Little by little I was able to maneuver the chair so that I could actually "dance" again using my upper body to control it. The wheels are my legs now you want to see?"

"Yeah!" said Kellie.

Sal called to the female dancer sipping water across the room. "Juanita let's spin." Juanita put on some music with a Latin rhythm and the two began to "dance" actually float. If Sal wasn't lower than her you wouldn't notice the wheels.

"Thanks Juanita." Sal rolled over to the CD player and turned it off.

"You can do anything you want as long as you love it and sometimes a tragedy gives you the will to do what you love no matter what. Kellie, the way I see it you are really lucky."

"Why am I lucky?" said Kellie pointing to her stump.

"For one you are learning from the best," said Sal looking at his wife, Eileen. "Secondly, you won't be in a chair for the rest of your life. You will get your new leg and be able to walk again."

"If it was only that easy," Kellie rolled her eyes and looked down at the floor.

"Sal, Kellie just had her first session with the leg and it was tougher than she thought it would be to walk with it," said Eileen explaining why Kellie was so down.

"Eileen what is it that you always say, "I can take failure, but failure can't take me, right?" said Sal.

"That's right." said Eileen.

"Easy for you to say." said Kellie.

Sal turned to Mrs. Jones and asked "when do the kids have their first school dance?"

"I think Homecoming is in January, right Kellie?"

"Yeah ma," said Kellie.

"By then you should be jumping puddles with your new leg. So I'll tell you what, you bring your date here and I'll show you my best dance moves for free."

"Really?"

"A dancer never lies. However, we do step on a few toes occasionally." Sal said as he winked at Mrs. Jones and Eileen.

"Thank you so much, Mr. uh Sal. That's so cool!"

"That's very generous, Mr. Amaranti. You are so kind," said Mrs. Jones.

"Anything to help another athlete," said Sal. He shook Kellie's hand. This time when they left the studio, Kellie had a determined smile on her face.

CHAPTER TWENTY

REVENGE ISN'T ALWAYS SWEET

On the first day of school, Kellie couldn't wait to slip on her tights and mini skirt. She hadn't worn a skirt since before her accident since she always wanted to cover herself by pinning the remainder of the pant leg up over her stump.

Now with the prosthesis she could wear anything. She was walking great and only needed a few sessions of physical therapy. She slipped on her beloved boots and fastened the ID bracelet her mom got her. As she sat on the bed, she looked down at the letters engraved on it: "Miss Risk". Yup, she was definitely taking a risk today.

Then she reminded herself that she never read Mary-Chris' note. She hadn't been to the creamery since the swim meet, but sent her a thank-you note through the mail. Mary-Chris said her parents wouldn't let her have a computer. She didn't even have television. Kellie, couldn't imagine her life without "Gossip Girl" and her computer.

She looked for the note in the box and in the bag, but it was gone. Kellie thought to herself, "It must have fallen out in the locker room. Damn I wonder what it said?" Kellie scratched her head worried, but realized it was probably a congratulations note. She really had to get to the creamery after school and thank Mary-Chris in person. Of course, it would also be a chance for her to show off her boots. This was the first day she would wear the prosthesis to school and start the year off strutting in with Maggie and Susan by her side instead of Mrs. Connolly, not that she didn't like the woman. Mrs. Connolly came to the house after Kellie's swim meet and gave her a hug. She brought with her a new bathing suit for Kellie and told her how proud she was. Mrs. Connolly said she would see Kellie everyday anyway because she got the high school secretary job she wanted. Kellie was happy for her and felt glad that she would be nearby.

Kellie was finally riding the bus like everyone else. The girls made plans to meet outside in the parking lot after their buses dropped them off.

"I'm so nervous. I hate the first day," said Maggie to Susan and Kellie.

"You're nervous? What if my leg falls off?" laughed Kellie.

"It's suctioned on there girl. If a New York cab knocked you over, it wouldn't come off," said Susan, trying to be helpful, but it didn't work.

"Well, here goes nothing." said Kellie as they adjusted their pocketbooks and back packs; they finally entered the lobby of the school.

The crowd seemed to turn and look at them all at once. A girl named April ran up to Kellie. "Hey, where's your wheelchair?"

"I don't need it anymore. I got a prosthetic leg."

"Really and I heard you are training for the Olympics or something. Can I come watch you compete in a meet sometime?" April was a nice girl, but a little nosy.

"Sure. I'd like that." Kellie looked at Maggie and smiled. "School isn't going to be that bad this year I guess."

Then Kellie felt a big push as if a line backer hit her from behind. She fell to the ground, landed on her back pack and started gasping for air as everything turned fuzzy and then faded to black. One boy accidentally kicked

Kellie in the head when he tripped over her. As he fell he yelled "Help!"

Maggie and Susan were ahead of Kellie since April slowed her down. They didn't even see her fall until they heard the cry for help.

Everyone merged into a circle. Kellie started to awaken. The room was spinning and then she heard a familiar voice say "That's what you get for stealing my boyfriend." Jade stood over Kellie and kicked her prosthesis. "Oh, you've fallen and you can't get up now, huh? I guess it was better being a tripod stuck in a wheelchair." Jade bent down and her eyes seared into Kellie's, "Your new leg doesn't seem to be working Bionic Woman. Better go to the mechanic and get a new part."

Susan and Maggie waded back into the crowd trying to get to Kellie. Eric sprinted forward pushing people in his way. He saw Hunter Davis running for the door and jumped on his back. Mrs. McCoy was in the main office getting her mail and talking to the principal when she looked out the glass window into the hallway. She heard more shouts than usual and saw two kids throwing punches. She and the principal ran to the scene. The principal broke up the boys and Mrs. McCoy ran right to Kellie.

"Are you okay, Kellie. Are you hurt?"

"I dunno."

"Let's call an ambulance for you just in case." Mrs. McCoy saw Kellie's face turn red.

"Oh, I don't want to do that." Kellie looked at Maggie in embarrassment.

"Can I go with her, Mrs. McCoy?" Maggie hoped the answer was yes.

100

"Of course," Mrs. McCoy pulled out her cell phone and called 9-1-1. "Okay kids back to class, except for you Jade Santiago. The principal is not done with you yet."

"But I didn't push her. I only yelled at her. Hunter was the one who pushed her." said Jade with a fake smile. Meanwhile, the principal was a little preoccupied. He was trying to tear Eric off of Hunter Davis' back. Eric was probably half the weight of Hunter, but he was mad and the weight difference didn't seem to matter as he beat Hunter to a pulp. Soon they were separated.

"I bet you put him up to it," shouted Eric at Jade. "Kell, are you OK?"

Just then the ambulance parked outside the door and the medics came rushing in with a stretcher. They did a preliminary exam on Kellie and said she seemed fine, but since she blacked out they decided to put her on the stretcher and take her to the awaiting ambulance. The medic opened the school lobby door when a boy shouted "Wait!"

It was Eric, who ran beside the stretcher. His face was cut up a little, but Maggie saw Hunter being escorted to the principal's office. Hunter looked a lot worse than Eric.

"I never knew she would be that mean. You have to believe me. Jade was mad when we last talked and asked me about you, but I told her we were just buddies. I'm so sorry."

"It's not your fault. You're not a psychic, but if you are can you tell me if I win the Paralympics?" Kellie tried to laugh but a cough came out instead.

"I don't know about that, but I guarantee there is a pizza with pineapple, anchovies and hot pepper flakes in your future."

"Really and with extra cheese?"

"Yeah, really and maybe a new boyfriend too."

"It's about time," said Maggie rolling her eyes.

Kellie smiled and waved to him as the stretcher was lifted into the ambulance and left for the hospital.

"Did he just say he would be my boyfriend?" said Kellie to Maggie.

"Yes and you know what that means?"

"What?"

"If the two of you get married, you're name would be a color - Kellie Green."

Kellie laughed. "I always thought it was the prettiest color in the crayon box."

Maggie held her hand. "It is," she said.

The next day as Kellie got off the bus she felt different. Kids were funneling out around her racing to get to their lockers while she just stood outside staring at the front doors of the school. Her green backpack slid off her shoulder and tumbled to the ground.

She wondered will this year be any different without her wheelchair in the way. Was she prepared for the changes ahead? Two things she knew were for sure: she didn't have to worry about Jade or Hunter Davis today. Jade got suspended for a week and Hunter was arrested for assault and battery. Since he committed a felony, Hunter was expelled from school.

Jade's father, Dell came for her disciplinary meeting that afternoon completely drunk. He started swinging his fists at the principal and Mrs. McCoy. Then he started beating Jade. They called the police and Jade's uncle Jorge arrived to find Jade cowering in the corner while Dell took shots at Jade's head calling her "a no good whore". The principal and Mrs. McCoy were trying to pull him off of her with no success.

Jorge arrested Dell and promised Jade she could come live with his family. She would be safe there and he would get her psychological help.

Kellie feared Jade's return to school next week. But she hoped her life would get better and she would get the help she needed.

Sora and Mary-Chris came over to Kellie's the night she was released from the emergency room. Sora said she felt guilty because she was the one, who told Jade about Kellie getting a new leg. "I saw it on your Buddybook page first."

"I was so hoppy for you," said Sora with her thick Japanese accent. "I didn't know Jade would do dat. I thought she be hoppy too. I didn't think she would hurt you."

Mary-Chris found out that Kellie never opened the letter because she lost it in the locker room. Mary wrote it as a warning. Her parents won't let her have a computer and she didn't tell Susan because Sue was sick with fever and couldn't come to work for two weeks before she gave Kellie the boots.

Kellie never mentioned the note in her thank you card to Mary-Chris so Mary thought she needed to stay out of it. A little embarrassed, Mary told Kellie that she lit a candle at church for her and prayed anyway. "Whatever, it still didn't do any good," Mary-Chris said.

"Sure it did. Both of you are my guardian angels. I didn't deserve your friendship either, M.C.," Kellie smiled at Mary-Chris realizing she misjudged her. "I'm really sorry. I didn't realize how much you both cared about me.

That's true friendship and I'm glad to have you in my corner."

Mary-Chris clasped her hands and knelt down to pray. "God, this is M.C. speaking." Mary-Chris smiled towards Kellie. "People think I have your toll free number so I just want to ask you to protect me and my friends and ask you to bless our friendship always, Amen."

The next day, Kellie stood at the entrance to Port Jervis High again. But she knew that nothing in her backpack could have prepared her for all of the events that happened this summer. School was more than just about acing a test or getting through the next chapter in the textbook.

"Hey, shake your tail feather, girl." said Maggie, "we're gonna be late."

"You go in. I'll be there in a second."

Maggie rolled her eyes. "Whatever." Kellie saw Maggie join up with Susan inside the lobby.

"Will this be a different year without my wheelchair? And will I be able to handle it" said Kellie to herself.

The lobby door opened and Eric walked outside.

"Hey Kell, what are you waiting for? Come on in."

Kellie lifted her green backpack off the ground and slipped it over her right shoulder. She hugged the folders she couldn't fit in the backpack against her chest and stood firmly on the side walk in her new boots. She took a deep breath and walked towards Eric. He put his arm around her and they walked into school and towards their future together. It was then Kellie realized life's problems should be tackled the way she approached her swim competitions. So she promised herself from now on she would face her fears and take risks, dive into the deep-end and try her best. That's all it will take to be victorious.

ABOUT THE AUTHOR

Amy Berkowitz is a columnist and journalist for a newspaper in upstate New York. As a girl, she admired and enjoyed books by Judy Blume, Beverly Cleary, Peggy Parish and Miriam Chaikin. Their books got her through many tough times as a young girl and shaped her as a writer. She hopes "Down, But Not Out In High School" will do the same for her readers and reinforce the idea that everyone faces challenges, but it's how you deal with them that counts. This is the author's first young adult novel. Please feel free to contact her at amywriter@hotmail.com.

ABOUT SISU BOOKS

Sisu Books is a small press founded in 2009 by Michael J. Worden. Sisu Books is committed to publishing unique, regional, historical and specialty books by regional and local authors.

Sisu is a Finnish word meaning determination, strength of will, perseverance, mettle and sustained courage. For additional information on Sisu Books and to see the current list of titles available visit www.sisubooks.com or write:

Sisu Books
PO Box 421
Sparrowbush, New York 12780

a Sisu Books publication
www.sisubooks.com

LaVergne, TN USA
13 June 2010
185942LV00004B/19/P